WHEN THE LAST DANCE IS OVER

Other Books by Glen Ebisch

To Breathe Again
The Crying Girl
Ghosts from the Past
Grave Justice
A Rocky Road
Unwanted Inheritance
Woven Hearts

WHEN THE LAST DANCE IS OVER

•

Glen Ebisch

AVALON BOOKS
NEW YORK

Published by Avalon Books,
an imprint of Thomas Bouregy & Co., Inc.
New York, NY

Library of Congress Cataloging-in-Publication Data

Ebisch, Glen Albert, 1946–
When the last dance is over / Glen Ebisch.
p. cm.
ISBN 978-0-8034-7463-5 (hardcover : acid-free paper)
1. Women editors—Fiction. 2. Murder—Investigation—Fiction. 3. New England—Fiction. I. Title.
PS3605.B57W47 2012
813'.6—dc23

2011033934

PRINTED IN THE UNITED STATES OF AMERICA
ON ACID-FREE PAPER
BY RR DONNELLEY, HARRISONBURG, VIRGINIA

Chapter One

Bradley Morgan, better known as Buster to his friends and most people in the town of Arbella, Connecticut, came out the front door of the country club and stood for a long moment under the portico, breathing in the cool night air. He'd had too much to drink this night, as he did on most nights, but he was hoping as always that the walk across the parking lot to his car would clear his head for the short drive home. Not that he had to worry about the police arresting him for driving under the influence, not in the town of Arbella, where he had lots of friends. If the police should happen to pull him over, he'd be recognized instantly, and the worst that would happen was that he'd be driven the rest of the way home and have to pick up his car at the police lot in the morning.

It's nice to live in a town where people know you, Buster thought to himself. The idea made him feel warm and content, so much so that he almost went back inside for a nightcap. But he knew that if he got really and truly drunk at the club, Brick might hear about it, and the last thing he wanted to face first thing in the morning at work was a bawling out from the boss.

Making a conscious effort to propel himself forward, and stumbling only slightly as he stepped off the curb, he headed out across the parking lot with all the grim determination of the early pioneers. He knew where his car was parked, because he always parked it under the same light so he'd have no trouble finding it. As he walked diagonally across the lot, Buster praised himself, as he did every night, for having this amount of foresight. But a worrying hint of confusion entered his mind as he drew closer to the car that he thought was his. Leaning against the front fender of the vehicle with her back to him was a young woman. At least, he guessed she was young because of her slender waist and the blond hair down to her shoulders. She was looking across the parking lot as if there were something fascinating that only she could see in the lines of parked cars.

For a moment, Buster's alcohol-soaked mind tempted him to steal up behind her, clap his hands over her eyes, and shout, "Guess who?" He always liked to hear girls scream; invariably, it gave him the opportunity to put his arms around them and offer comfort and apologies. But then he recalled that the last time he had tried that, over two years ago in this very same parking lot, the girl, who couldn't have weighed more than a hundred pounds, had turned out to be a third-degree black belt in some Asian martial art. She had elbowed him smartly in the side of the head and then given a remarkably powerful roundhouse kick to his solar plexus. All of this ended with him on his knees, trying to catch his breath, followed by his vomiting a prodigious amount of alcohol and bar snacks onto the asphalt. Even more humiliating were the scornful smiles of the ambulance attendants who took him to the hospital to be checked over.

No, this time I'll play it by the book, he thought, and he complimented himself on his prudence.

He walked up to the rear fender of his car, checked the license plate to make absolutely certain that it was his, and then cleared his throat theatrically to warn the woman that he was there. She gave no indication that she had heard him. Buster walked as far as the driver's door.

"Can I help you, miss?" he asked.

There was no response.

"I need my car, so you'd better get off the fender," he said, deciding that this politeness had gone far enough.

Again, she didn't turn or give any sign that she had heard him. Buster considered starting the car, and if that didn't move her, he'd just back up and let her fall on her butt. But the memory of his unfortunate past experience in the parking lot had made him doubly cautious. With his luck, she'd turn out to be the deaf daughter of a wealthy member who was a lawyer, and he'd find himself sued for grievous bodily injury. Buster didn't know for sure what that was, but it sounded like something to be avoided. So instead of getting in the car and driving on his carefree way, he walked forward until he was only three feet behind the woman.

"*Excuse me,*" he said, hoping the sarcasm would make it seem like he was the one in control of the situation.

When there was still no response, he wondered if she really was deaf. He took another step forward and touched her gently on the shoulder.

She spun around so fast that Buster stumbled backward

and almost fell. Then he stared at her for a long second, trying to understand what he was seeing.

The left side of her face and neck were covered in some kind of dark liquid that had run down over the front of her white dress. *Blood,* Buster suddenly realized. It was blood. His eyes slowly moved in the direction of her raised right hand. He saw the long, thin-bladed knife at the exact moment she plunged it into his left shoulder. The pain made him cry out. Buster knew he hadn't said a word, just some kind of grunting, animal sound. He glanced at her face and saw the lips curl into a malicious smile. The hand with the knife went up again.

Buster knew with absolute certainty that if he didn't move, he would die right there, tonight, in this parking lot. With a greater effort of will than he had previously demonstrated at any time in his adult life, Buster turned and began to run. After staggering for the first few steps, he picked up speed until he was cruising along at what he knew had to be his fastest pace since he'd run eighty yards for a touchdown at the Thanksgiving Day game during his senior year at Arbella Consolidated. It didn't hurt that he clearly pictured the girl chasing him with her knife upraised.

When he finally reached the front door of the club, he pulled it open and rushed inside. Only when he could see some of his friends sitting at the bar did he dare to take a quick glance behind. There was no one there. Surprise mixed with relief as he caught his breath, not taking his eyes off the front door. When several minutes had passed and everything seemed safe, he slowly walked back to the glass door and looked outside, sure that she would suddenly pop up in the center of his field of vision.

But as he stared out into the parking lot, he saw nothing

unusual. Buster counted the lights until he came to his own car. As far as he could tell from this distance, she appeared to be gone. *If she had ever been there at all,* Buster suddenly thought. That moment of doubt got him wondering if all his years of drinking had finally caught up with him. He'd heard of guys suffering from hallucinations due to a lifetime of too much booze, but Buster had always figured that he had a long way to go before he reached that sad state. But what if he was wrong? What if this was the beginning of a slow brain rot that would eventually deprive him of his grip on reason?

He stood staring out the window, almost in tears over the impending loss of his mind. Then, as the adrenaline subsided, Buster became aware of a pain in his shoulder. He raised his left hand and watched, awestruck, as blood dripped off the ends of his fingers. For a moment he felt relief, knowing that the girl really had been there and that his sanity was intact. He smiled at the thought that he could happily go back to drinking.

Then he fainted.

Chapter Two

Marcie sat in the chair by the side of Amanda's desk and fidgeted. It wasn't like Amanda to call her into the office first thing on a Monday morning. A weekend of e-mails were waiting to be read and answered, and plans for the upcoming week were usually discussed over bag lunches together in the conference room. It also wasn't like Amanda to ask her into the office and then leave as soon as she got a phone call, promising that she'd be right back. Marcie was tempted to return to her own office down the hall, where work awaited her, but Amanda's unusual nervousness and somber formality had rubbed off on Marcie, and she stayed where she was.

The offices of *Roaming New England* magazine occupied an old house along Route 1 in Wells, Maine. The window in Marcie's office looked out on the traffic that passed by at a fairly rapid clip on a Monday morning as people either rushed north for their jobs near Portland or headed south in the direction of Boston and its suburbs. Amanda's office, however, had an oversize window in the back of the building that afforded her a view across the marshes to the rows of houses along the ocean. From this distance, Marcie thought, they appeared like the plastic models used on electric train layouts, and the blue of the ocean could have been a skillfully painted backdrop. A restful view and the sun working its way higher in the sky promised a bright early April day.

Marcie tried to relax, and she even found it possible to stop her staccato tapping on the desktop just as Amanda sailed back into her office. She settled gingerly into her desk chair and began twisting the beads around her neck, staring at Marcie the whole time as if trying to gauge whether she was ready to hear the news. Marcie returned to tapping.

"Would you please tell me whatever you have to say?" Marcie finally exploded. "All I'm doing is sitting here imagining the worst—that I'm about to be fired."

She had expected Amanda to laugh and tell her how silly she was to even have that thought. But Amanda seemed not to have heard her.

"So am I fired?" Marcie asked softly, the tension obvious in her voice.

"No, of course not," Amanda replied, shaking her head as if suddenly returning to the present. "What's happened is that Greg has quit."

Marcie almost smiled in relief, but she controlled herself, because she knew that Amanda and Greg were close friends. Marcie suspected that maybe Amanda would have turned it into more than a friendship, except for Greg's frequent references to a mysterious girlfriend back in the Boston area. Three months ago, he had been transferred to Boston, to help the parent company that owned *Roaming New England* get its new cooking magazine off the ground.

"I thought he was coming back after they hired a managing editor for *Eating New England* or whatever they finally decided to call that magazine," Marcie said.

"*Culinary New England,*" Amanda corrected. "Instead, they offered Greg the job, with a substantial increase in pay, but he turned them down."

"Wouldn't they let him come back here?"

"They gave him the option. But some friends of Greg's from his newspaper days have just started a small political magazine in Boston. So he decided to go with them."

"I'm not really surprised. Are you? After all, he'd worked in the newspaper business before he took over as managing editor here. As an experienced journalist, he must have felt that he was slumming by working on a magazine that focuses on arts, leisure, and anecdotal stories."

Amanda nodded but didn't seem to be paying attention. "They've given me Greg's job," she announced nervously.

"Congratulations!" Marcie said, reaching over and enthusiastically squeezing Amanda's arm. "You certainly deserve it. You've really been the managing editor since Greg left."

"Thanks," Amanda said, giving Marcie a small smile that quickly disappeared. "Unfortunately, they didn't promote you to my job. They felt that since you have only been here two years, you aren't ready to take over as senior editor."

" 'They' being Sam Peabody?" Marcie asked.

"Who else?" Amanda said.

Sam Peabody owned the magazine, along with several other publications, and he was known for being very hands-on when it came to business decisions, especially those involving money. He normally stayed in the corporate headquarters in Boston, but he had visited their office once. A thin, gray-haired man with an unhappy expression, he had looked suspiciously at Marcie when she was introduced, as if her meager salary were going to bankrupt the company. His only comment to her was, "Keep up the good work," in a tone that implied that she would never be able to do so.

Marcie sighed. She had sort of hoped for a minute that Greg's leaving would put her in Amanda's job, but she had to admit that she really wasn't quite experienced enough for a senior editor. So she decided to act like a mature professional.

"Okay. I can see why they might think that way. I'm the first to admit that I've got a lot to learn."

"But on the bright side, they have promoted you from assistant editor to associate editor. And along with that comes a small raise in pay. I'm not sure how much it will be. I'm still waiting to hear from Sam about both of our raises. That's why I rushed out to take that call from him just now, but he wanted to talk about other things."

"A raise would be great," Marcie said, several uses for the extra money springing quickly to mind. "Who's going to have the job of senior editor?"

"They're not going to fill the position. The way the economy is now, I guess they don't want to spend the money."

"We need more than one editor. You'll be tied up going to Boston to meet with Sam, working with Joe in layout, and trying to increase advertising."

"What we need and what we're going to get are two different things. Sam says we'll just have to learn to do more with less."

"That's easier said than done."

Amanda shrugged. "We don't have a choice. But one thing that makes it more possible is that Sam wants to cut back on the size of the magazine."

"What's he planning to take out?" Marcie asked with a sinking feeling in the pit of her stomach.

Amanda gave her an encouraging smile. "Don't worry, it isn't the Weird Happenings section. In fact Sam likes that because it's cheap. What he wants to cut are the travel articles where we spend so much to reproduce those photos on glossy paper. As Sam keeps reminding me, paper doesn't grow on trees."

"He's going to have to put some money into pictures with that new food magazine. People want to see appetizing photos of food, so they can see what the mess they made was supposed to look like."

"Well, I guess we're going to be subsidizing that new magazine for a while."

"That's not fair," Marcie said.

Amanda shrugged. "It's not supposed to be. It's business. And at any rate, it's good news for you, because Sam wants to expand Weird Happenings. He thinks it brings in readers, and it doesn't cost much because we only have to pay a pittance to the authors of the stories. The biggest expense is paying your travel expenses. So from now on, we'll have to justify every receipt we turn in to headquarters."

"I could always camp out in a tent," Marcie said, grinning.

"Don't say that in front of Sam. He'll take you seriously. What he said to me is that the national motel chains are too expensive, and we should utilize the local motels, which are cheaper and will allow us to experience the true ambience of the place."

"Ambience meaning thin sheets, rough towels, and an overall odor of mildew."

"Nobody said road trips were supposed to be fun."

"Speaking of travel, do you remember at the end of last week I asked you if I could take Thursday and Friday off to travel down to Connecticut to check out the lead I got on a story?"

Amanda nodded. "I said that you could if we were finished editing for the next issue."

"I'll easily be done with that by Wednesday. So can I go?"

"Remind me again what this is all about?"

"A friend of mine from college, Steve Rostow, called me and said that the ghost of a murdered girl is haunting the town where he lives."

"What town is this?"

"Arbella, Connecticut."

Amanda frowned. "Never heard of it. Wasn't the *Arbella* the ship that the founders of the Massachusetts Bay Colony took over here?"

"I suppose. Anyway, this is a town out in the eastern part of the state."

"And who is this murdered girl?"

"Steve said her name was Melissa Harrison. She was murdered back in 1991. She was only seventeen. Her throat was cut."

Amanda shivered.

Marcie nodded. "I know what you mean. It's horrible to think about. Anyway, they found her body by the side of the road that went from the high school toward the town. This was on the night of the senior prom."

"And she was at the prom?"

"According to Steve's research, she and her boyfriend came to the prom is a rented limousine with two other couples that were friends of hers. Melissa was seen dancing at various times throughout the evening, but she left early after having a fight with her boyfriend. She was still wearing the prom dress when her body was found."

"Has the ghost of this girl been haunting the town ever since 1991?" Amanda asked.

"No, it only started a month ago."

"A month ago!" Amanda rolled her eyes. "Not exactly a well-established ghost."

"That means we can be the first to write about it," Marcie said, the enthusiasm obvious in her voice.

"We aren't running a true-crime magazine here. Weird Happenings is supposed to be about stories of supernatural events that occurred in the past."

"Melissa's murder is in the past, and we've done a couple of stories that started in the past but involved contemporary murders."

"I know. We worked together on one of them, and the last one almost cost you your life."

"But readers want to know about things that are currently happening. A ghost that hasn't been seen in fifty years is old news. According to Steve, there have been three sightings of Melissa's ghost in the past month."

"Why do they think it's this girl's ghost?"

"The way she's dressed. She's wearing a prom dress with blood all over the front of it."

"So somebody who knew the history of the town saw something strange one night and decided to liven things up by declaring it the ghost of Melissa Harrison. And due to the power of suggestion, anyone who sees a shadow at night is turning it into a ghostly girl."

"The first person to see her was stabbed."

"To death?" Amanda asked.

"No, but he needed stitches. The point is that she's using a long-bladed knife like the one that was used on her. And the guy stabbed was one of the guys in the limo with Melissa that night."

Amanda pursed her lips. "I have to admit that it's starting to sound interesting. How are you going to set this story up? Are you going to begin with some background about what happened in '91, then have a few paragraphs toward the end about what's going on today?"

"It's Steve's story, but that's probably the way he'll do it. He's a good writer. We worked on the college paper together."

Amanda grinned. "Oh, so maybe it's not the ghost that's taking you to Arbella, but the chance to see Steve again."

Marcie shook her head. "Steve and I were just friends. I never thought of him as anything more than that."

"Maybe you didn't, but Steve could have different ideas."

"I doubt it. Steve's interest in me begins and ends with getting his story published. He teaches high school history and works on some local free historical paper called the *Arbella Archives*. But he's always wanted to be a journalist, so I think he sees this as a way out of spending his life teaching the Civil War to high school juniors."

"Tell him not to give up his day job," Amanda warned. "Publishing is hard work, made interesting only by its insecurity."

"So, can I go?" Marcie asked.

"You can go down there for a couple of days and see whether there really is a story in all of this. If you think there's something worth publishing, tell Steve we'll pay him our usual rate, but emphasize to him that we want more about the supernatural and less about the murder of that girl." Amanda paused and stared hard at Marcie. "And remember, you are not to get involved in any way with an ongoing investigation. I don't want you confronting a murderer like you did the last time."

"I won't," Marcie said, crossing her heart.

"I wish I could believe that," Amanda said.

"And I'll stay in the cheapest place I can find."

"Maybe you could stay with Steve," Amanda said, giving her a sidelong glance.

"I don't think so," Marcie said. "He lives in his parents' basement."

Chapter Three

Steve Rostow put his feet up on the gray metal desk he used in the *Arbella Archives* office, a storefront in a half-abandoned strip mall a few blocks from the center of town. Putting his feet up allowed him to momentarily think of himself as being like one of those newsmen you'd see in the old movies: tough guys who lived to drink whiskey straight, run around with brassy blonds, and break the big story. Someone who would fearlessly investigate until he found the truth, no matter what risks were involved. It was a day-dream that Steve found far easier to imagine here than in the room he still occupied in his parents' basement. It was also easier to imagine it now that he had a real story to investigate.

He smiled to himself. *I've got a great story developing right here in town, I've just about got a contract to write about it for a regional magazine, and I'm going to see Marcie again.* They had gotten along really well when they worked together on the college newspaper. She was the only person in college he thought might write even better than he did.

Thinking about writing inspired him to put his feet down and pull out his notes from the battered briefcase. As he looked over the sheets of yellow legal-size paper covered with his precise printing, he smiled to himself again at how complete and colorful his descriptions were of each appearance of the ghost. He patted himself on the back for persisting in the face of adversity, like any good journalist would.

And there had been plenty of adversity, at least by local standards. Buster had point-blank refused to talk to him, even threatening to do him physical harm when Steve had confronted him in the parking lot of Brickmore Industries, where Buster worked. This wasn't surprising, because his boss, Roger Brickmore, had been Melissa's date for the prom, and he wouldn't want the murder investigation resurrected. Buster's refusal to talk didn't really matter, because Steve had an old high school friend who was one of the EMTs called to the country club the night of Buster's collapse. When Buster first regained consciousness, he had told anyone who would listen about what he had seen in graphic detail, so Steve had a pretty good description of the event.

The people who had made the other two sightings were personally more forthcoming, but their stories were less exciting, because neither one of them had been actually attacked by the ghost. Mary Watkins, who had gotten in touch with him because she was a friend of his mother's, had seen the ghost running across the parking lot of the Super Save More at nine o'clock at night. Mrs. Watkins probably never would have realized it was the ghost if the figure hadn't stopped and stood still right under one of the parking lot lights not more than fifteen feet away from her startled eyes. Steve paused over his notes for a moment to consider getting Mrs. Watkins to drive to the parking lot again and pull into the same space, so he could measure exactly how far away she had been from the ghost. But Steve decided it probably wasn't worth the trouble. Mrs. Watkins hadn't been very keen on talking to him in the first place, and she kept asking him what all this had to do with the *Arbella Archives*. Since the *Archives* would never publish anything as sensational as this, Steve had put her off with vague assurances that she was providing valuable background information for a historical article he was writing.

The other sighting came from a high school boy named Kyle Root, and Steve had heard about this via the school gossip line. He had a passing acquaintance with Kyle from supervising afternoon detention, which Steve, like all the younger teachers, had to cover for a month during the school year. Kyle was an almost permanent fixture in detention, because he was always coming to school late or getting caught by the high school police officer for smoking on school grounds. In fact, that's exactly what Kyle had been doing when he'd seen the ghost. He'd been standing behind a large rock that prevented him from being seen from the school building, having a smoke before showing up late, as usual, for his second-period English class. While enjoying his cigarette, he had happened to look out into the woods that surrounded the school and spotted a figured flitting from tree to tree.

It was at this point that Steve had asked him if his

cigarette was of the illegal kind. Kyle swore, rather unconvincingly, that he never touched weed. And that what he was smoking was the garden-variety menthol kind.

Taking up the story again, Kyle described how the figure had come closer and closer to the edge of the woods right in front of him. He had stood there, trying to figure out what was going on, until she had finally stepped out from behind a tree not twenty feet away. One look at the blood down the front of her dress and the long knife in her hand, and he had dropped his cigarette and run as quickly as he could back to school. Considering that Kyle had a bad smoker's cough and had skipped gym class for most of the year, Steve figured he hadn't been very fast, and the ghost could have easily caught him. But when Kyle turned to look behind him, before rushing into the school and breathlessly reporting what he had seen to the principal's secretary, the ghost had disappeared.

Steve put his feet back up on the desk and stared across the room, which held six other desks identical to his own except for a different pattern of dents in their metal sides. Three people had seen the ghost, he thought, but only Buster had been attacked. And he was the only one who had been at the prom the night Melissa Harrison was murdered. To Steve's mind, this seemed more than just a coincidence.

The phone rang. Steve quickly picked up and in his special newsman's voice announced that the caller had reached the *Arbella Archives.*

"Is that you, Steven?" a woman asked.

"Yes."

"This is Sally Maes. You've probably heard your mother speak of me."

Since Steve tried not to listen to his mother's long conversations about her many friends, he had no idea who the speaker was. But he was too shrewd a journalist to let that be known.

"Of course I have," he said brightly. "What can I do for you?"

"I think it's more what I can do for you. Your mother mentioned to me that you're planning to write a story about this ghost that's supposedly running around town. Is that right?"

"Yes. Have you seen the ghost?" Steve asked, unable to keep the excitement out of his voice.

"Better than that. I work as a nurse in the emergency room in General Hospital. They just brought in somebody who apparently was attacked by the ghost."

"Who is it?"

"Her name is Penny Schuster."

The name rang a bell, but just to be sure, Steve leafed quickly through his notes until he found the list of people who had traveled together with Melissa to the prom. There she was, he thought with a silent shout of triumph. Penny had been Buster Morgan's date for the night.

"How badly hurt is she?"

"Cuts on her hands and forearms. I heard the police say something about defensive wounds. The doc is going to clean them up and see if any need stitches. I guess she won't get out of here for another hour."

"Can I get in to see her?"

"Nope. The security guard takes his job seriously. But if you stand outside the door to the emergency room, I'll tip you off when she's about to leave. You could try interviewing her in the parking lot."

"I'll be there, and thanks, Mrs. Maes."

"A pleasure to help. Your mother always says what a fine boy you are. You don't find many twenty-five-year-olds who stay around the house and help their mothers with chores."

Steve mumbled his good-bye. It was bad enough that he lived in his parents' house. Did his mother have to brag about it to everyone who would listen?

Ten minutes later, Steve drove his classic Honda Civic into the emergency room parking lot and was lucky to get one of the few spaces reserved for visitors. Grabbing his pen and notebook, he hurried up to the glass doors and peered inside. A young woman was sitting behind a counter looking at a computer monitor while at the same time talking to an older woman in scrubs who was leaning over the counter. Steve tapped lightly on the glass. The older woman stared at him for a moment, then walked toward the door.

"You must be Steve," she said, stepping outside. "It's been years since I've seen you. I don't think I'd recognize you all grown up."

Steve smiled politely. "Hi, Mrs. Maes. Is Penny Schuster still being treated?"

The woman nodded. "But I don't know that you'll get much of a chance to talk with her."

"Why not?"

"After I called you, Roger Brickmore showed up with the chief of police and pretty much kicked everyone out of the room except the doc taking care of her cuts. I imagine they'll be escorting her home."

"How can they get away with that?"

"You know who Brickmore is, don't you?" Mrs. Maes continued. "He owns the old Brickmore textile mill, guess it's called Brickmore Industries now, and it has something to do with computer technology. His father was a big contributor to the original building fund for the hospital, and the son pretty much paid for the new wing. So when he says everyone out but the doc, there's no argument from anyone. Plus, he has the chief of police with him."

"Chief Grundfeld," Steve muttered, half to himself.

Mrs. Maes nodded. "I've never seen him come down here for a minor assault like this, and you'd think Mr. Brickmore would have better things to do in the evening. I wonder why they care so much about this ghost business."

"Because Brickmore was there the night that Melissa Harrison, the girl who supposedly has come back as a ghost, was murdered. In fact, he was her date."

Mrs. Maes' eyes flew open. "He was!"

Steve smiled at the effect he had produced. "And Grundfeld was at the prom that night as well. He and Brick are old friends from high school."

"It's hard to imagine them having anything in common. Mr. Brickmore is so polite, while Chief Grundfeld is so rough."

"Their paths separated after high school. Brick went to Yale, like his father and grandfather, and Grundfeld went to community college. When Brick came back to town, Grundfeld was already on the police force, but I'll bet being friends with the wealthiest guy in town has something to do with his becoming chief of police before he was thirty."

"Maybe," the woman said doubtfully. "But Arbella is a nice town."

"Only if you don't dig beneath the surface."

Mrs. Maes looked ready to argue, but just then a small procession came out the door of the emergency room.

Steve recognized the chief of police as the man in the lead even though he was wearing civilian clothes. Behind him was Roger Brickmore, who had his left arm around the waist of a woman whose hands and forearms were completely white with bandages. The chief was a big man with a bald head and a thick neck. What had once been a muscular body had thickened around the middle, but he still gave the impression of a force to be reckoned with. Roger Brickmore was of average height and rather slight, with a full head of black hair mixed with just enough gray to give him an air of maturity.

Steve rushed to position himself on the sidewalk, where they'd have to pass close to him.

"Ms. Schuster," he called out when they were still a few feet away, "I'm Steve Rostow with the *Arbella Archives.* Would you tell me where you were when you were attacked by the ghost?"

The woman glanced in his direction and opened her mouth as if to answer when Chief Grundfeld veered toward Steve. He lowered his shoulder and struck Steve solidly in the chest. Steve grunted and fell backward onto the lawn.

"Excuse me," the chief said and kept walking without pause.

"Ms. Schuster has nothing to say," Roger Brickmore added, looking down at Steve with an apologetic smile.

Steve lay there for a moment, getting his breath back. A real newsman would have decked the two of them, Steve thought, feeling acutely aware of his limitations, although on some level he knew that in real life trying that would have just gotten him arrested. He scrambled back to his feet, pointedly ignoring the hand up that Mrs. Maes offered.

"Well, that was certainly rude," she said.

"Still think this is a nice town?" Steve asked her, as he carefully brushed off the seat of his pants.

Mrs. Maes watched the police chief help Penny Schuster into his car, then turn to shake hands with Brickmore. "Let's just say that I'm a bit less certain about it than I was a minute ago."

Chapter Four

Marcie smiled to herself as she passed a sign that read ENTERING ARBELLA: A NICE PLACE TO BE. She wondered if that modest claim was still true now that the town had its very own resident ghost. Underneath the sign was a set of placards for the variety of fraternal and civic organizations with a presence in town. *I'll bet Steve isn't making himself very popular with these folks by going around town digging up information about the murder of Melissa Harrison,* Marcie thought, *and I won't have many fans either once they realize that I plan to publish Steve's story in a regional magazine. Maybe I'd better keep a low profile.*

The scattering of houses on both sides of the road began to thicken, and in a few minutes, the buildings took on a larger and more commercial flavor. When she reached the town green, Marcie knew she was in the center of Arbella. A developing headache behind her eyes reminded her that she'd had an early breakfast because she'd wanted to finish a few things in the office before leaving. So she decided that, since it was almost noon, this was a good time to have some lunch. She pulled into a town parking lot off the green, then walked back to the center. The downtown area seemed to run about three blocks in a north-south direction. Marcie decided to head north, hoping that she'd soon come upon a place to eat. She'd gone past a couple of fast food places on the way into town, but she didn't think that even Sam Peabody would begrudge her a decent meal, as long as it wasn't too costly. After two blocks of walking, her search was rewarded when she came upon a corner store window with lettering that said SUSAN'S RESTAURANT, a simple name for a simple place. Marcie glanced through the window and saw that several of the tables were already occupied, which she took as a good sign. She went inside and sat at a table for two in the corner.

A young waitress immediately came over, handed her a menu, and asked what she wanted to drink. She opted for lemonade, since the temperature was warm for early spring and she'd worked up a thirst on her walk. When the waitress came back, Marcie ordered the turkey club sandwich, then opened the local newspaper she'd purchased from the box along the way, and began to read. A few minutes later, the waitress returned with her sandwich, which came with chips and a nice side salad. The turkey was fresh and tasty, and the salad didn't contain any of the usual boring iceberg lettuce. So Marcie happily ate and read, slowly working her way through the paper.

The newspaper came from the nearest large city, so very little of the news pertained to Arbella. That's probably why Marcie's eyes were drawn to a small piece on the bottom of the fifth page that had an Arbella dateline. All it said was that a local woman had received knife wounds the previous night during what the police described as a possible hold-up attempt. Her name was Penny Schuster, and the wounds were not life threatening. She'd been treated at Arbella General Hospital and released. Marcie sat back in her chair and wondered whether the so-called thief happened to look like a girl who had been murdered on prom night. She could imagine that the police might prefer to keep that information to themselves as long as possible for the sake of the town's image.

"How was your lunch?" asked a woman who wore a name tag that said SUSAN. She was older than the waitress, probably in her early forties.

"Excellent," Marcie said. "Are you the owner?"

The woman smiled and nodded.

"How long have you been in business?"

"Ten years in June."

"Did you live in Arbella before that?"

"Oh, sure. I grew up here."

"Did you know a girl named Melissa Harrison?" Marcie asked cautiously.

The woman's mouth tightened into a straight line. "Everyone who lived in Arbella twenty years ago either knew her or knew about her."

"Because she was murdered?" Marcie asked gently, hoping to keep her talking.

Susan nodded. "Her being murdered was bad enough, but *when* it happened made things even worse. I was in her class in high school. Can you imagine what it was like when they found her body on the night of the prom? That was all anyone could talk about for weeks. It threw a real wet blanket over our graduation. People were even afraid to have parties, because somehow it would be disrespecting her."

"Did you know her well?"

"I knew who she was, but we didn't hang out together. All I know is that in her senior year, she was in Brick's gang."

Marcie gave her a puzzled look.

"Roger Brickmore—everyone calls him Brick—was the son of the richest guy in town. His family pretty much ran things around here for a long time. That's not quite so true now, because there are other companies where you can work, but from what my dad told me, in the old days, you either worked for Brickmore Textiles or you didn't have a job."

"Who was in this Brickmore gang?"

"Besides Brick and Melissa—although to be fair, she didn't really hang out with the rest of them, just with Brick himself—there was Buster Morgan, Penny Schuster, James Kerr, and Kim Tyler." Susan grinned. "We used to say that you had to be thick as a brick to be part of the gang."

"Why is that?"

"Brick ran it like a little king. You only got to stay in the gang if you did what he said."

"So what did happen on the night of the prom?" asked Marcie.

Susan looked at her suspiciously. "Are you some kind of reporter?"

"I work for *Roaming New England* magazine."

The woman started to move away from the table.

"Jeez, I don't want to get quoted in a story."

"Please," Marcie said quickly, "I won't use your name. This is just for background information."

She shook her head. "If Brick ever found out that I'd told you this much, I'd find myself out of business in a week."

"He has that kind of power?"

Susan nodded.

"Why would he care so much about an old story?"

The woman looked around, checking to see if they could be overheard, and then she moved closer to Marcie.

"He was suspected of killing Melissa, but the police could never prove anything. Brick has spent his life living down that accusation, and he'll destroy anyone who tries to bring it all up again." Before Marcie could say anything more, Susan walked quickly back to the kitchen.

Since Steve didn't get out of school until three o'clock, they had set three thirty for the time Marcie would meet with him at the *Arbella Archives* office. Having a couple of hours to kill, she decided to drive around town. She wanted to find the road that led out to the high school, the same road where Melissa Harrison's body had been found. When she paid her bill, Marcie asked the waitress how to get to the high school. The young woman, who couldn't have been more than a year or two out of high school herself, gave Marcie clear directions.

As she drove northward, out of the downtown area, Marcie glanced at the map to his office that Steve had sent her. Like everything he turned his hand to, it was painstakingly done, with physical landmarks drawn in and all the road names carefully printed. This made it easy for Marcie to see that driving out to the high school would take her right past the strip mall where the *Arbella Archives* had its office. She decided to scope it out, so there'd be no trouble finding it at three thirty.

Less than a half mile out from the center of town, she saw a row of stores and a faded sign that said NORTH ARBELLA MALL. She pulled into the parking lot and looked up and down the line. A small convenience store anchored the left end of the mall, while the right boasted a Laundromat. In between, punctuated by empty storefronts, were a Chinese restaurant, a bank, and a store with a sign above that said THE ARBELLA ARCHIVES. Marcie drove down the row and parked in front of the office. The sign had been reused; Marcie could see the faint outline of LEO'S PIZZA: THE BEST PIZZA IN THE WORLD, which had been inadequately painted over. Not very impressive, Marcie thought, but the physical structure didn't necessarily say anything about the quality of the publication. She'd give Steve the benefit of the doubt.

She pulled out of the mall and headed further north on a street appropriately labeled North Main. The waitress had told her that she would see a sign pointing to a road that branched to the right, indicating the way to the high school. After Marcie headed onto the proper road, she found that the roadside was mostly given over to woods, and there were no buildings on either side. The ideal place to attack someone, Marcie thought. After driving about three hundred yards, she went over the crest of a small rise, and suddenly in front of her appeared Arbella Consolidated High School. It was larger than she had expected. Part of the building looked like it had been constructed forty years ago, and as she drove through the parking lot, Marcie spotted a cornerstone right next to the front entrance that said 1963. Having attended a number of different schools due to her father's military career, she had a good eye for the age of school buildings. Another section of the building, which appeared to have been added a couple of decades later, had a slightly different shade of brick siding.

As she pulled out of the school lot and headed back the way she'd come, a second question occurred to her: *why did they have the senior high school prom in the school gym?* Granted, she'd heard of this sometimes happening in the West when there was no restaurant nearby that had the capacity for a large group, but Arbella seemed like the kind of town that would boast at least one banquet hall in the vicinity. She made a mental note to ask Steve about that.

Marcie checked her watch and saw that it was almost three o'clock, which was the check-in time at the motel where she was staying, the Arbella Motel. Hoping to avoid being called on the carpet by Sam Peabody for running up expenses, she had chosen a small local motel rather than one of the more expensive chains out near the highway. In Marcie's experience, motels named after their location were frequently a disappointment; the owners' lack of imagination in selecting a name for the place was often equaled by their lack of inspiration in running it. Similar to the danger of eating in a place called *Mom's.*

But the rates were very reasonable, and the Arbella Motel was located just two miles past the turnoff for the high school, close to downtown but not right in the heart of things. *If this Roger Brickmore is as paranoid as the woman back at the restaurant thinks he is,* Marcie thought, *it might turn out to be better staying in a more out-of-the-way location, for the sake of privacy.*

Marcie drove back on the road that led to the high school, noting once again how deep woods ran right up to a steep gully that defined the edge of the road. When she got back to the fork, she turned right, heading farther out of town. Two miles later, a sign appeared on the right announcing THE ARBELLA MOTEL, with a vacancy notice hanging underneath it. Marcie turned in the driveway and paused. The motel was one row of maybe twenty units, each with a door opening right out to the parking lot, an old-fashioned design that still existed in many of the less touristy areas of New England. Three or four cars were scattered around the lot, so Marcie figured there were probably lots of vacancies. The center unit had a sign over the front door that said OFFICE. Marcie parked right in front of the sign and went inside.

The lobby was small, barely large enough for the two small wicker chairs and a table. A rack of tourist brochures filled out the corner. The rug was dark and dated, and the walls were covered with knotty pine, giving the room the shadiness and smell of a clearing in the forest. Marcie approached the counter. No one seemed to be around. She could see through the open doorway that there was a smaller room in the back that looked like a kitchen. She tried calling out "hello" in case someone was there, but got no response. A bell sat on a cardboard sign affixed to the counter with dirty masking tape saying RING BELL FOR SERVICE. Marcie pushed the bell, which gave a nerve-jangling ring that reverberated sharply off the knotty pine, but no one came rushing out of the back to see who was there. Marcie turned to go back outside, hoping to find an employee cleaning one of the units. But before she reached the front door, it opened and a slender woman of about her own age with long blond hair rushed in. She stopped suddenly with a startled expression, as if a customer wanting service was the last thing she expected to see.

"Can I help you?" she asked.

"I have a reservation. My name is Marcie Ducasse."

She wore a name tag that said LISA on her short-sleeved shirt, which was open to reveal a red tank top underneath. A tattoo peeked out from her upper left shoulder when she reached under the counter for a list of reservations. Marcie noted that her arms were muscular, as if she were an athlete. She might have asked, if the closed expression on Lisa's face didn't give off an aura of *mind your own business.*

"How long will you be staying?" Lisa asked in a challenging tone, as if long stays were not encouraged.

"A couple of days, at least. Is there any problem keeping my room if I decide to stay a little longer?"

"I guess not. But we have to honor our reservations first."

"Well, you certainly don't seem very busy," Marcie said impatiently, tired of the woman's rudeness.

"It gets busier over the weekend."

"I see," Marcie said, not quite managing to keep the doubt out of her voice.

Marcie filled out the registration form while Lisa ran her credit card. When Marcie handed the completed form across the counter, the woman carefully scrutinized it, then asked to see Marcie's license, as if she suspected her of being a terrorist intent on destroying the peaceful town of Arbella.

"Are you here for business or pleasure, Marcie?" the girl asked, giving her a long look.

Nonplussed at being interrogated, Marcie took her time while signing the credit slip to frame an answer.

"For both, I guess. I have a little bit of business to conduct, and I've never been to this part of Connecticut."

She could tell that Lisa wanted to ask what kind of business she did, so Marcie reached over and snatched up the key that the woman had placed on the counter, hoping that getting out of the office quickly would end the questioning. Lisa's right hand gave a reflexive move as if she wanted to pin Marcie's hand to the counter before she made her escape, but Lisa held herself in check.

"Have a nice stay," she said with a thin smile. "Unit ten is to the left. Park right in front of the door."

Marcie nodded and exited the office, wondering what had just happened. For a moment she entertained the idea that Roger Brickmore had somehow found out where she was staying and directed Lisa to keep an eye on her. But that kind of thinking was just too paranoid, Marcie decided. *Probably Lisa simply has an odd personality,* she thought, as she pulled her car up in front of unit ten, *and likes to play mind games with customers.*

She pulled her suitcase out of the trunk and opened the door to her unit. They still used heavy metal keys at the Arbella Motel—no fancy cards for them. Marcie wondered how many copies of that key had been made over the years. Probably enough to render the locked door worthless. And at any rate, Lisa would have a master key. Marcie decided to keep the security chain on whenever she was in the room and to secure her laptop and anything else with personal information in the trunk of her car whenever she left the room. She chided herself for being an alarmist but decided that her past experiences on the road justified a certain amount of caution. Maybe after talking to Steve, she'd decide that this was all unnecessary, but being in a strange town with no knowledge of the local situation made it prudent to err on the side of safety.

Marcie pushed the door open with her shoulder and lugged her suitcase into the room. She tossed it up on the bed and took a quick look around her home for the next few days. The room was spacious. There were two double beds, each covered by an identical faded bedspread. An older television sat on an imitation wood table along the opposite wall. On the wall between the beds was a large painting of a stream meandering through a woodland scene—the kind of art people bought for its size rather than its artistic value—and every wall was covered with the same knotty pine paneling as in the office. The room had a closed-in smell, as if no one had stayed there for weeks. Since the large front window didn't open and the one at the back of the room was taken up with an air conditioner, Marcie went into the bathroom and shoved open the small window over the toilet. She stood there for a moment looking out and suddenly saw Lisa dart out across the twenty feet of mowed lawn along the back and into the woods. A figured stepped out from behind one of the trees and took her arm. All Marcie could see was that it was a man. They stood there talking, their gestures sharp and urgent, and then the man glanced over his shoulder, back toward the motel. Marcie felt that he was looking right at her, so she ducked out of sight below the window. When she dared to glance out again, they were gone.

Marcie went over to the sink, ran the water until it was hot, scrubbed her face, and dried it thoroughly with the thin, scratchy towel provided. Then she went back into the bedroom, put the security chain on the door, and sat down to think. But it didn't take much thinking for Marcie to figure out that with Steve's story of a ghost, Susan's fear of Roger Brickmore, and Lisa's odd behavior, something strange was going on in the town of Arbella.

Chapter Five

Marcie pulled into a parking space near the front door of the *Arbella Archives.* It was five minutes before their three thirty appointment, so Steve would already be there. One of the things she remembered about him from their time together on the school paper was how organized he was. He had a much more mature approach to keeping a schedule than most college kids, whose view of showing up for meetings tended to be hit-or-miss. That was one thing he and Marcie had in common. Having been raised by a father in the military, her idea of being on time was showing up at least five minutes early.

She got out of the car, being careful to lock it, and went up to the glass door of the office. A sheet had been posted showing when they would be open. A glance showed her that someone was in the office on mornings three days of the week and on afternoons two days. Maybe not a sign that the business was thriving, but as Marcie knew from working at *Roaming New England,* most work could be done on a home computer and sent in via e-mail.

Getting advertisers could be done in the same way or by telephone. There was no reason for an operation such as this, which relied heavily on volunteers, to require extensive office hours.

She pushed open the door and went inside. At first all she saw were short rows of gunmetal gray desks. Then, out from under one of them in the second row, a figure emerged.

"I just dropped my pen," Steve said, waving the object as if he needed to prove the claim. Looking embarrassed, he smiled and walked toward her, bumping his hip on the desk right in front of her and staggering slightly.

They ended up facing each other, both pausing for a brief moment as if unsure how to greet the other. A handshake seemed too formal, a kiss too intimate. Finally, by unspoken agreement, they settled for a hug.

"It's great to see you again, Steve," Marcie said.

She looked at him carefully. Although they had caught up on the last four years over the phone when Steve called about the story, Marcie believed that seeing a person gave a more honest picture of how he was doing than words ever could. Steve was still tall and lanky, with arms and legs that seemed to move in all directions when he walked. His slightly goofy smile was as infectious as ever, but his face seemed older, a little sadder, as if the last few years had drained away some of his exuberance.

"You look great, Marcie. Have you lost some weight since college?" he asked, then rubbed his hands together nervously as if that had been too personal a question.

"Some," Marcie answered. Since working for *Roaming New England,* she had, in fact, lost quite a bit of weight, something she attributed to being happier than at any other point in her life. But she didn't like to talk about it, because that implied that weight was an important aspect of who she was, and Marcie didn't believe that.

"And you've got a great job. I've been reading Weird Happenings for a year now. You're doing fine work."

"How did you come to see my column?"

"I read all the regional magazines; it gives me ideas for things to write about in the *Archives*."

"You should have given me a call or sent an e-mail sooner. I've often wondered what you were up to."

"Yeah, well, you sort of see how it is," Steve replied, spreading his arms wide, inviting her to look around at his sad domain.

"Everybody has to start somewhere when it comes to writing. And you don't just do this; you're also a high school teacher."

"Yes. And there are lots of times when I actually enjoy teaching. The problem is, it's not my . . ."

"Passion?" Marcie said.

"Exactly. You know what I was like in college, always talking about how someday I'd be working on a newspaper or magazine, or maybe writing copy for a television news show. Well, when I graduated, I sent out my résumé everywhere in New York and Boston. When nothing came of that, I went back to college and got certified to teach. Like my mom always says, at least it's something to fall back on." Steve rolled his eyes as if he'd heard this more than once.

"I know how hard it can be. I spent my first two years out of college doing technical writing for an auto-parts distributor—talk about boring. There's only so much you can say about a spark plug. But somebody I'd worked with heard about this job at *Roaming New England* opening up and sent me an e-mail. I fired my résumé in to them right away and got the job largely because I had some professional writing experience, even if most of it was about the internal combustion engine."

"So you're saying that if I'd stuck with it a little longer, maybe I'd have something in writing myself?"

Marcie shook her head. "No, what I'm saying is that if you want to be a professional writer, then you have to keep doing it, even if the work is boring and doesn't pay much. And by working here, you're doing that. This is a job that will look good on your résumé, and your background in history could qualify you for any number of writing positions."

"Sometimes it's hard to think of this as a job, since I don't get paid."

"Is everyone here a volunteer?"

"No. The manager is on salary, and the person in charge of advertising is on commission. The rest of us do it for the love of the work."

"At least you're still writing. That counts. If nothing else, it's a good learning experience."

"I suppose so," Steve said, not looking completely convinced but more cheerful. "Why don't you come into my imaginary office, and we can talk about the story?"

They headed back toward the desk that Steve had been under when Marcie walked in. When they were a few feet away, Steve pretended to open an imaginary door and graciously gestured for Marcie to enter. He pulled a real chair over next to his desk for her.

"The money isn't much, but the perks are amazing," he

said, settling down in an office chair that sent a large protesting squeak around the room.

"I can see that," Marcie said with a grin. "I haven't had a chance to look at a copy of the *Arbella Archives*. What kinds of things do you publish?"

"We list all the local public activities for the month, and there are columns by a few of our regulars on medicine, finance, and the environment. I always have a piece about some event in local history. We usually take a couple of nostalgia articles where someone writes about a long-deceased family member or a fond remembrance of childhood. Of course, since we give it away for free, we have to get most of the local merchants and businesses to advertise, and that takes up the rest of the space."

"I wish *Roaming New England* could get by on just its advertising," Marcie said.

"The only way we can do it is by keeping our costs down. We print on inexpensive paper and use simple graphics. I do a good part of the layout work as well, so I've learned a lot about cutting corners."

"You see what I mean about your having all sorts of valuable experience," Marcie said.

"I get it," Steve said. "Now let's get down to our story."

Marcie smiled to herself, because the Steve who had been editor of the college paper always used that phrase as a way of showing that the time for small talk was over.

"Let me cut right to the financial part first," said Marcie. "All we can offer you is two hundred dollars for the story. That's our usual payment, and things are kind of tight right now, so I doubt I can get you more. Sorry."

Steve waved away her apology. "That's two hundred

more than I've ever earned here, plus I'm not doing this for the money. What I want most for myself is the credit of being published in a well-known regional magazine. The other reason I'm doing it is to help the town."

"You mean to help it get out from under the thumb of this guy Brickmore?"

Steve's eyebrows rose. "You work fast. Where did you hear about him?"

Marcie described her encounter with Susan, the restaurant owner.

"Yeah, lots of people in town are afraid of him, just like they were afraid of his father and his grandfather. And I have a feeling that this ghost story might be a way to loosen the Brickmore grip on this town." Steve paused and pulled on his lower lip as if there was something more he had to say.

"What is it?" Marcie asked.

"The thing is that if this really does turn out to be a sensational news story, I'd like it to have more exposure than appearing four months later in *Roaming New England*. I have a friend who works on the *Boston Globe* who says he'll get the story published over my own byline."

"And there's a local paper, too, isn't there? The *Arbella Beacon* or something like that."

"Yeah, but they're too afraid of Brickmore to publish anything that might make him look bad. They haven't published the truth about the two attacks that happened so far."

"Two? I thought there was only one."

Steve quickly filled her in about the assault on Penny Schuster.

"Getting back to the *Boston Globe* issue, if you're asking whether we'll agree to let you have the story published first in a newspaper, I guess that's okay. Your story for us will have to place more emphasis on the ghost-story part and less on the political side of things."

"That's a deal," Steve said, reaching across the desk and shaking Marcie's hand.

"So fill me in on the story so far," Marcie said. "You only gave me a thumbnail sketch over the phone."

Steve rolled back in his chair and put his feet up on the desk. Marcie automatically did the same. This was the way they had always sat when discussing stories at school. Somehow it felt natural.

"Well, like I told you on the phone, Melissa Harrison was found dead along the road leading up to the high school the night of the senior prom. She had arrived at the prom with her date, Roger Brickmore. Two other couples shared the limousine with them: Bradley—better known as Buster—Morgan brought Penny Schuster, and James Kerr brought Kimberly Tyler."

"Were these people all friends?" asked Marcie.

"I don't know how much they liked each other, but from what I've been able to find out, all of them except for Melissa made up Brick's gang of followers that had pretty much been together throughout high school."

"What about Melissa?"

"She didn't hang out with the group. She went out with Brick on his own, and that had only been going on since the start of the spring semester."

"Did anything significant happen during the prom that involved Melissa?" Marcie asked.

"That's been hard to find out. The Brickmore group wouldn't talk to me. I've questioned several other people who were there, and from what I've pieced together, Melissa was at the prom until around eight thirty. Several people saw her arguing with Brick just before that. After eight thirty, there were no sightings of Melissa until her body was found along the road at ten o'clock by some people leaving early to head down to the shore."

"What about Brick? Was he seen during that time period?"

"Three of the members of his little crew claim to have seen him several times between eight thirty and ten o'clock. No one else questioned by the police could remember for sure."

"How did you find that out?"

Steve winked. "I have a friend on the force."

"Did the police suspect Brick?"

"Sure. I guess they were working on the principle that the person closest to Melissa would be the one most likely to have killed her. And he had a reputation for being pretty wild. But when Brick produced three witnesses who swore to having seen him when the crime was committed, and his father got him the best legal counsel money could buy, the police just gave up."

"Did they have any other suspects?"

"Not really. Some people figured it was a serial sex killer who just happened to be in the neighborhood. But Melissa hadn't been raped, and there were no crimes of that type reported anywhere in the area before or shortly after Melissa's death."

"I have a couple more questions."

"Fire away."

"Why did they have the prom in the school gym? I would think it would have been held at a restaurant with a banquet facility."

"Usually it would have been. But there was a big graduating class that year, over four hundred, and the only place in town that could hold a function for that many had burned down back in December. Brickmore senior offered to pay for transportation to a country club banquet room twenty miles away, but that never got off the ground. The kids didn't want to go so far away, and the school board didn't want to be that obviously in debt to Brickmore."

Marcie nodded. "I drove up the road to the high school and noticed that there are thick woods along either side of the road. So why didn't the killer just drag Melissa's body off into the underbrush? She might not have been found for quite a while, and that would have made it harder to establish when she was killed."

"The police wondered the same thing. They figured that maybe the murderer was planning to do just that when the car full of kids came along, so he ran."

"Could Melissa have been in a car with anyone? Were there any tire tracks?"

Steve shook his head. "And the kids who found the body didn't see a car driving away. The police figured that for some reason Melissa decided to walk home from the prom, and somebody followed her and killed her."

Marcie frowned. "Party shoes aren't exactly made for walking."

"Melissa lived only half a mile away from the high school, so she might have figured it was manageable. She didn't have any shoes on when her body was discovered, but the shoes were found nearby."

"Why didn't she just call home for a ride?"

"Nobody was home at her house until ten o'clock," Steve said. "From what I've heard, her folks beat themselves up over that for years. 'If only I'd been home,' that sort of thing."

"I can imagine. What were Brick and Melissa arguing about at the prom just before she left?"

"We only have Brick's word for any of this, because nobody overheard them. But according to him, Melissa accused him of cheating on her with another girl." Steve leafed through his notes. "Cindy Gower is her name. Brick denied that there was anything going on between them, and Cindy backed him up when questioned by the police."

"Then why would Melissa have made the accusation? Especially on the night of the senior prom. No girl wants to spoil that by calling her boyfriend a cheater unless she knows it's true."

"According to Brick, Melissa frequently thought that he was cheating on her. My guess is that she was probably right most of the time. Of course, that's no guarantee that she was right this time."

"No, but she must have had some pretty convincing evidence about something to get her to take off and start walking home."

Steve shrugged, clearly not as convinced that Melissa had reasoned things through. *Maybe he thinks women are highly emotional creatures who do things for no good reason at all,* Melissa thought with a flash of anger. *But no,* she reassured herself. *Steve might not have a lot of experience with women, but he never seemed prone to stereotyping them.* She'd give him the benefit of the doubt.

"I wonder why Melissa's ghost suddenly showed up now?" Melissa asked.

"You don't really think there's a ghost, right?" Steve asked with a nervous smile.

Marcie thought about explaining how complicated her views of the supernatural had become since working on Weird Happenings, but she decided it was too early in their reestablished relationship to hit him with that.

"I don't believe everything people tell me on the job," she said, reassuring him with a smile. "What I mean is, why has someone suddenly decided to dress up like Melissa and start running around town attacking people?"

Steve shrugged. "If we knew the answer to that, I think we'd have the whole thing solved."

"Has anybody new come into town recently who would be a good suspect?"

"Arbella is pretty small, but it isn't so small that you can keep track of every newcomer. Plus, our ghost could be staying outside of town but somewhere in the vicinity. From what I've heard from my source, the police have checked every motel and bed-and-breakfast within ten miles, and anyone coming close to being young and blond has been questioned. Of course, whoever is doing all this is probably disguising themselves pretty well."

"And at the same time managing to look quite a bit like poor Melissa."

Steve nodded.

"How do you know?" Marcie asked suddenly.

"Know what?"

"Know that she looks like Melissa?" Marcie frowned. "I guess what I'm asking is, who first recognized the ghost as being Melissa Harrison?"

"I think it was Buster. After all, he was the first to see the so-called ghost, and he knew Melissa pretty well."

"Can you check to be sure?"

Steve nodded, swung his long legs off the desk, and

pulled his folders of notes out of the battered briefcase. He turned to the beginning of one of the files and began scanning them. A few moments later, he looked up at Marcie.

"According to what I found out from the guys on the ambulance who responded to the call from the country club, once he regained consciousness, Buster started shouting about a weird girl who tried to kill him. Sometimes he rambled on about zombies. I don't think he made a whole lot of sense; he was probably in shock. But my police source said that when they went to interview him in the hospital, he said that it was the ghost of Melissa Harrison."

"Who is this police source you keep referring to?" asked Marcie.

Steve checked his watch. "My guy called half an hour ago and should be coming along any minute now."

As if on cue, the front door opened, and a young woman in a police uniform walked inside. She was slender and several inches taller than Marcie. Even though she was wearing a heavy utility belt, her hips still looked slim, Marcie thought with a trace of envy. When she removed her hat, Marcie could see that her dark hair was pulled back into a bun, making her look rather stern. That disappeared when she saw Steve and greeted him with a big smile, making Marcie wonder whether her interest in Steve was personal. Steve stood up, returning her smile.

"Hey, Jena, there's somebody here I'd like you to meet."

Steve introduced them and Marcie learned that her name was Jena Conway. Steve went on for a few minutes about how helpful she had been for his research, having provided him with information from the police reports of the incidents. Marcie nodded, feeling that she was definitely the third person making the crowd.

"Marcie was just asking me how the idea started that the so-called ghost was Melissa Harrison. Do you know?"

Jena sat on the edge of the desk across from them and stared up at the ceiling. "When they brought Buster in, I got the call at home to meet the chief at the hospital. He was getting a ride in from a friend, but I was supposed to bring him home." She turned to Marcie. "I've been Chief Grundfeld's driver for the last few months. When I got there, the doctor had just finished getting Buster stitched up, and he'd been moved into a room. I guess they'd given him something to help him sleep, because he was pretty drowsy."

"Did you ask who had attacked him?" said Marcie.

"Sure. He told me that it was a zombie dressed up to go to a party." Jena smiled. "To tell you the truth, if Buster hadn't had that big bandage on his shoulder, I wouldn't have taken him very seriously. We've all had to stop Buster one time or another for driving under the influence."

"And he still has a license?" Marcie asked.

Jena lips tightened and she turned a little red. "Buster has friends. So we just drive him home."

"I'd like to have a friend like that," Marcie said. "He must have a lot of influence."

"He's the chief of police, Charlie Grundfeld," Steve said. "More indirectly, the influence comes from Roger Brickmore."

Marcie nodded, not wanting to embarrass Jena further.

"So he was going on about a zombie?" Marcie said.

"Yeah, I was ready to just write up a report saying that

the patient wasn't in enough possession of his faculties to be interviewed when Chief Grundfeld walked in."

"What did Grundfeld say?" Steve asked.

"He listened to Buster ramble on about this girl with a knife and blood all over the front of her dress. Finally, he walked over to the side of Buster's bed and grabbed him by the arm. He must have squeezed pretty hard because Buster's eyes popped open wide. Then the chief said, 'Did it look like Melissa Harrison?' "

"What did Buster say?" Marcie asked.

"He said, 'Melissa, yeah that's who it was. It was Melissa.' I didn't think there was anything strange about that, so I said to the chief, 'Do you want me to pick up this Harrison girl for questioning?' He gave me a funny look, and said, 'That would be a good trick, Conway. Harrison is dead.' "

"So it was the chief who got Buster thinking that it was Melissa?" Marcie asked.

"I guess so," Jena said. "I never really thought about it before. Why would the chief assume it was her?"

"Because maybe he and all of Brickmore's friends are still feeling more than a little guilty about what happened to her. When they see someone parading around with a cut throat, it all comes back to them that they lied to help Brick," said Steve.

"This doesn't get us any closer to knowing who's pretending to be Melissa's ghost," said Marcie. *If it* is *a pretense,* she mentally added.

"Well, it was nice meeting you," Jena said, shaking hands with Marcie. "I guess I'd better be on my way. I dropped the chief off at city hall half an hour ago. He said the meeting would take an hour, but you can never be sure." She walked to the door, then paused. "Just a bit of advice. If I were you, I'd just write this whole thing up based on what you've got right now, and then leave it alone."

"Why's that?" asked Steve with a grin. "Marcie and I aren't afraid of a ghost."

Marcie thought saying that was a sure way of pushing your luck.

"Because if you start digging into the Melissa Harrison murder," Jena said, "some pretty powerful people in this town are sure to come after you. And that's no ghost story."

With a final wave, she opened the back and disappeared.

"She's got a good point," Marcie said after a minute. "I don't have to live in this town, but you do. Get the wrong person mad at you, and you might even lose your teaching job."

A look of doubt passed over Steve's face. Then he sat up taller in his chair, and a look of defiance took its place.

"I've got to follow this story wherever it goes," he said a little too loudly. Then he added, more softly, "It's my last chance to really become a writer."

Marcie wasn't sure how much to say. She wanted to urge caution, but at the same time, she didn't want to offend her friend by suggesting he lacked courage. And to be honest, she understood what he was saying. This could be the kind of story that would help launch his writing career.

"Since I've been doing this job, I've seen quite a bit of violence. And it seems to me that a story about a ghost that goes around stabbing people has the potential to become pretty dangerous, especially because of the involvement of the richest man in town and the chief of police. Personally, I'm just not ready to go through something like that so soon after my last bad experience. Even if you aren't afraid, I think I'd like to be cautious until we discover more about what's going on. Would you do that for me?"

Steve stared at her for a long minute, as though trying to gauge the sincerity of what she was saying. He didn't want to be patronized. He knew that he tended to come across as a nerd, someone who could research and write but was not a man of action. He was determined to prove that evaluation of him was wrong. That he could be an investigative reporter who followed the story wherever it went. But when he looked at Marcie, he could tell that she really was frightened at the prospect of taking on this story. So he gave what he hoped was a gallant smile.

"We'll follow whatever approach you want," he promised.

Chapter Six

Marcie parked her car in a public lot at the south end of town and began walking up the street, keeping a careful eye on the shop windows. She was looking for Penny Schuster's beauty salon, which was called Penny's From Heaven. After Jena left the *Arbella Archives* office the day before, Marcie and Steve had discussed how to proceed based on what was least likely to get them in trouble with Brickmore or Chief Grundfeld. Steve really wanted them to directly question all those who had been part of Brick's inner circle at the prom, but he admitted that they would probably be unwilling to talk and that it might lead to a conflict with Brickmore or Grundfeld. Marcie proposed a plan that would get them some of the information they wanted by the use of guile rather than confrontation.

The day before, Marcie had proposed that she would call Schuster's salon and try to make an appointment to have Penny do her hair Friday morning. Pretending to be a visitor staying outside of town at the home of friends, Marcie hoped that she might get Penny to open up to a sympathetic stranger about the events of the other evening. The one flaw in the plan was that she might have to wait several days for an appointment, but she was pleasantly surprised to get right in for ten o'clock on Friday morning.

In the middle of the next block, Marcie saw a sign decorated with a picture of large golden pennies falling out of the sky like miniature flying saucers. Marcie opened the door, causing a bell to jangle over her head loudly enough to make her jump.

"Hi. How're you doing?" a voice called from inside the shop.

Marcie peered into the shadows, trying to see where the voice had come from. Then the lights went on, and a short blond woman came toward her. She was wearing designer jeans that had fit her twenty pounds ago and a red blouse that barely spanned her ample chest. Her face showed vestiges of the pert prettiness of someone who had been a cheerleader twenty years before.

"I'm your ten o'clock," Marcie said.

"Lucky you weren't any earlier, or the door would have been locked. You're my first appointment of the day."

Marcie didn't think a ten o'clock starting time indicated a thriving business. She was also surprised to see that the room was large, with six beauticians' chairs and a waiting room for a dozen customers. Did she happen to be there on a slow day, or had Penny expected her business to grow more quickly than it had?

"I'm Penny. This is my place," she said unnecessarily, given the name.

She gestured for Marcie to take the first chair on the right.

"You've never been here before, have you?"

Marcie gave her the story about being a visitor staying out of town.

"Yeah. I usually forget a name, but I never forget a head. And I certainly would never forget yours. It's not often that you see a head of such naturally curly hair. If you dyed it red, they'd call you Little Orphan Annie."

Marcie smiled politely while Penny gave a lengthy and deeply congested cough, suggesting that she was a heavy smoker. When she put a hand up to cover her mouth, Marcie saw the edge of the bandages on her arm.

"What happened to your arm?"

"Both arms really. I got attacked by a mugger the other night. He had a knife."

"That's really scary. Were you hurt badly?" Marcie asked.

"No. Two of the cuts needed a few stitches; the rest just needed to be cleaned up."

"Did it happen here in town?"

"Not right downtown." Warming to the story, Penny walked around to the front of the chair so she could look directly at Marcie. "I was taking my garbage out. It was around ten o'clock at night, and I put on the light over the garage. I'd just thrown the stuff in the can and was walking back to the house. All of a sudden this"—Penny paused—"big guy steps out of the shadows with a huge knife in his hand and comes right at me."

"My God! What did you do?" asked Marcie.

"I put my arms up when he started slashing at me. That's how I got these."

Penny unbuttoned her cuffs and revealed her two arms, which were bandaged up to the elbow.

"I would have fainted."

"I was too scared to faint."

"You were lucky you weren't killed."

"Don't I know it. The only thing that saved me is that the guy was kind of clumsy. He sort of stumbled the last time he came at me with the knife, and that gave me a chance to run around him and get into the house. Then I called the police right away."

"Did they catch him?"

"Nah. He was long gone by the time they got there."

"Funny kind of a mugger, though," Marcie said after a moment.

"What do you mean?" Penny asked.

"Well, you probably weren't carrying your wallet or purse when you went out to dump the garbage. So how could he expect to steal anything?"

A deep frown came over Penny's face, as if she weren't accustomed to dealing with puzzles. Then a smile of relief replaced it.

"Maybe he thought he could threaten me into letting him into the house. That would have been really terrible. He might have stolen all my dog miniatures. And who knows what would have happened to my toy poodle, Tricksy. She would have tried to defend me." Penny shook her head contemplating the horror of such a struggle. "She might have been killed."

Marcie shook her head. "It still doesn't quite make sense. Why would he attack you? He could just have waved the knife around and demanded that you let him in the house."

Penny paused for a moment. "Well, maybe he wanted to terrorize me, so I'd do whatever he wanted. When you see your own blood, you start to take things seriously."

"I suppose," Marcie said doubtfully.

Penny moved to the back of the chair as if to end the conversation.

"So what would you like done?"

"Just wash and a blow dry."

"Are you sure? You know, if I trimmed your curls just a little bit, it would give you a whole new look. Or we could try straightening your hair. Wouldn't that be a hoot?"

Marcie finally convinced the woman that she only wanted a wash and blow dry. A half hour later she was done, and no other customers had entered the store.

As Marcie paid, she glanced around the room and said, "This must be your slow time of the week."

"Nah, it's about average. People seem to space themselves out. But I usually get three or four a day."

"That doesn't seem like a lot for a big shop like this. Do other beauticians rent chairs from you?"

"No. They used to, but they moved on."

"It must be hard to make the rent."

Penny winked and stepped closer, whispering even though no one else was there. "The landlord is a friend of mine and gives me a break."

Marcie smiled. "Lucky you. But still, I hope business picks up soon."

"They've been saying that downtown is ready to take off ever since I've had the place."

"How long is that?"

"Fifteen years."

Marcie left the shop and walked to the corner. She looked up at the building that housed the beauty parlor.

It was impressive, made out of gray stone and taking up the whole block. She happened to be standing by the cornerstone on which she saw, elaborately carved, THE BRICKMORE BUILDING.

Steve sat in the faculty room trying not to stare at Kimberly Tyler, the third woman in Brick's group who had been at the prom aside from Penny and Melissa. She had smiled politely when he'd entered the room and said hello, then returned to grading papers. He rarely came into this teachers' lounge. The high school had three of them, and this was the one most often used by those who taught in the wing of the school where senior classes were held. Since Steve generally taught sophomores, along with the occasional junior class, he rarely ventured into this part of the school. He knew that he had to work fast. In ten minutes the bell would ring, and he'd have to rush from one end of the school to the other.

Although he knew who Kim Tyler was by sight, he had never spoken with her. The more senior and more junior teachers didn't generally socialize much. So now Steve was racking his brain, trying to find a topic of conversation that could be worked around to a discussion of Melissa's ghost. Not the easiest conversational gambit to formulate. He was also feeling guilty. He had just about promised Marcie last night that he would lie low so as not to antagonize Brickmore, but this morning he had awakened with the conviction that he shouldn't be so timid. He'd decided that perhaps the truly manly thing to do would be for him to take on the riskier interviews, allowing Marcie to be more indirect in her approach.

"Are you an English teacher?" Steve asked.

"Yes," the woman replied, glancing up from the papers she was grading.

"What are those essays on?"

Obviously more anxious about getting her grading done than in having a conversation, she replied, "These are junior papers. We're doing early American literature. They happen to be on Edgar Allan Poe."

"A fascinating writer," Steve said, leaning forward with excitement at this lucky opportunity. "It must be particularly interesting to be discussing Poe at the same time that there's a purported ghost running around town. I'm sure the students all want to discuss that."

"I don't know what you're talking about."

"I'm sure you've heard the same rumors I have, that the ghost of Melissa Harrison has been wandering around town. She even attacked Buster Morgan and Penny Schuster."

"Don't be silly."

"So you don't put any stock in the stories about Melissa's returning for revenge against the people who went to the prom with her?"

Kim Tyler went a bit pale. "Of course not. I don't believe in ghosts. Where are you getting this drivel from?"

"But you knew Melissa?"

"Of course. We went to high school together."

"Her death must have been a real tragedy."

"Anyone dying at that age is a tragedy," she snapped.

"But being murdered like that is particularly sad."

The woman turned her attention back to her papers. "I don't mean to be rude, but I have to get these done by next period."

"Of course. Sorry." Steve got to his feet and headed for the door. "But you've got to admit it's curious that all the people attacked so far were in that little group of six who went to the prom together. That would be Buster, Penny, Brick, Kerr, and yourself. Why do you think that is?"

"I have no idea," the woman said without looking up.

Steve tried to smile self-confidently, like those guys on television who get people to break down and tell them everything with one meaningful look.

"You know, you'd be a whole lot safer if you told me everything you know. Between us, we might be able to figure out who this ghost is and put a stop to the attacks."

"I'm not telling you anything, and if you don't get out of here, I'm going to report you to the principal and my union rep."

She glared angrily at Steve. It was a good glare, but he could tell that behind the anger there was fear. But not enough fear to get her to talk.

Chapter Seven

The man at the desk took his right hand from the keyboard of his computer and rubbed it across his brow. He glanced at his watch. Seeing how late it was, he began the process of turning off the computer. It was time to go home to dinner. He was amazed at how much of his time as a veterinarian was given over to paperwork. It was getting as bad as being a people doctor, with all the folks who now had medical insurance for their pets, which required the submission of countless forms. He had a part-time secretary who handled that sort of thing, but she was always falling behind on the billing, so he often pitched in himself after office hours. The work was rapidly reaching the point where he would need someone full time. He wasn't sure that Kathy, his current secretary, would be willing to take on more hours. She had a young family and needed to be home by the end of the school day.

Like I don't have children myself that I'd like to see once in a while, James Kerr thought bitterly. On the other hand, the success of a small veterinary practice, like any other small business, was directly related to its ability to keep down overhead. People were often willing to pay a large amount to take care of the family pet, but you still had to be careful not to price yourself out of the market, a definite risk with three other veterinarians in town. He couldn't dispense with his trained veterinary assistant or the high school boy who came around after school to clean. It was a good thing that the rent on this building was low, something he owed to Brick, the building's owner. Otherwise he didn't know what he would do.

James walked out of his office and down a short hall to his treatment room. He checked to make sure that the cabinets containing drugs were securely locked. Then he went in the back of the building to the room devoted to recovery and observation. There were only two animals there tonight. One was a cocker spaniel who'd had a large growth removed from his paw this afternoon. James squatted down to look into his cage and said his name. The dog's head slowly turned in James' direction, but his eyes were unfocused. Although the dog was still drowsy, James knew he would be fine in the morning. A white cat whose owner said that she wouldn't eat occupied the other cage. He'd see how she did in the morning, but suspected that there might be a bowel obstruction. He said good night to the animals by name, not sure whether it did much for them, but it always made him feel more in touch with why he had gone into the profession, something easy to forget after an evening spent filling out forms.

Shutting off all the lights and turning the heat down to its lower nighttime level, he opened the back door into the employee parking lot and stepped outside. He turned back to make sure the door had automatically locked behind him, then headed slowly across the parking lot to his car. A glance in the direction of the Dumpster that occupied the corner of the lot revealed that several boxes were scattered on the ground around it. It wasn't like Tim, his high school cleaner, to be so sloppy. With a sigh, James walked toward the Dumpster; he'd have to take care of it himself. The men would be there before dawn the next morning to empty the Dumpster, and they had made it very clear to him in the past that they simply dumped the metal box and never picked up loose items on the ground.

Opening the metal lid to the Dumpster, he picked up each of the boxes and threw them inside. As he walked around the side of the Dumpster to pull the lid back into place, she was suddenly there. The light in the corner of the lot showed the blood that had run freely from the wound in her throat and down the front of her dress. Even her light blond hair had been stained red in the front right above her forehead. Although James had heard rumors of the attack on Buster, he had disregarded them as the ramblings of an alcohol-soaked brain, and he understood the attack on Penny to be nothing more than a mugging gone wrong.

So when Kerr was confronted by the ghost, he asked, "Who are you?"

The figure smiled as if to say that he should know, and her right hand came out from behind her back brandishing a long, thin knife. Before he could react, the knife came down and he felt a sharp pain in the top of his left shoulder. He stumbled backward, but the girl moved relentlessly toward him. A instant later he felt a second pain, this one on the top of his right shoulder. He stood there for a second, his hands held out in front of him, fingers spread wide, to ward off more attacks. But his attacker paused, a ghastly smile on her face, as if she were enjoying his shock and pain.

Expecting her to move toward him with a lethal thrust to his abdomen or heart, he pulled his arms down and hugged himself. Eyes closed, he waited for the end. When a few seconds passed and nothing happened, he turned away from her, keeping his eyes closed, as if not looking at the apparition would make her go away, and then opening his eyes, he ran to his car. When he had locked himself safely inside and started the engine, he finally dared to look back. He saw nothing. As he pulled quickly out of the parking lot, he glanced at the side of the Dumpster, but no one was there. Except for the blood running down both his arms and the image seared in his mind, he could almost believe that this had all been a waking nightmare, a figment of an overactive imagination.

Chapter Eight

Five, six, seven, eight, nine, ten!" Marcie triumphantly concluded counting all the water-stain marks on the old white block ceiling of her motel room. She was hoping that there'd be no heavy rains during her stay for fear that the ceiling would end up as her blanket.

She had been working on her laptop all afternoon, polishing up a couple of pieces for a future issue of *Roaming New England*. By now, she was so bored that staring at the ceiling was more interesting than proofreading for the third time an article on the real estate deals struck by Ethan Allen of Green Mountain Boys' fame. Giving in to the inevitable, Marcie turned off her laptop, went into the bathroom, and splashed some cold water into her tired eyes.

As she rubbed the towel over her face, Marcie glanced out the small window over the toilet. Just like yesterday, she saw Lisa, the girl who worked at the motel, running across the back lawn. At the edge of the trees, staying just out of plain sight, was a man. As Lisa ran across the lawn toward the trees, she slipped and fell. The man moved toward her, then caught himself. A moment later, after seeing Lisa regain her footing, he stepped back into the woods. From where she was standing, Marcie could make out that he was a large man who was either bald or had shaved his head. He was wearing a denim jacket over a dark T-shirt and jeans. Marcie couldn't be sure, but he looked like the same man Lisa had met in the woods the day before. Once Lisa reached him, they both moved farther into the trees, and Marcie lost sight of them.

Marcie ran back into her bedroom and pulled her binoculars out of the suitcase. She hurried back to the window and focused them on the spot where the man had been standing. After a couple of minutes of waiting, her arms got tired and the glasses began to shake, so she put them down on the toilet tank and watched with just her naked eyes. Almost as soon as she put the binoculars down, Lisa reappeared. Marcie grabbed the binoculars and got them to her eyes just as the man followed Lisa a few steps out of the woods. His face had a blunt, hard look, not the sort of man you'd want to come across in a dark alley. He made a gesture, pointing with his figure toward the motel, and as he did so, he put his other hand on his hip, pushing back the denim jacket. Marcie saw something on his hip: a gun? a cell phone? The shadows of early evening made it hard to tell. Before she could get a second look, he was gone, and Lisa was running back to the motel.

Marcie returned the binoculars to her suitcase and sat on the edge of the bed. What was going on here? Her first thought, the other day, had been that Lisa was meeting with her boyfriend when she was supposed to be working, hence the secrecy. But the man she had seen today was clearly in his forties, a bit old for Lisa. And the way he had pointed looked like he was ordering her to do something. Some boyfriends could act that way, but on their brief acquaintance, Lisa hadn't struck Marcie as the kind of girl who would happily accept being pushed around.

Marcie glanced at her watch. She and Steve were going out to dinner later. He had gone home to change and, Marcie suspected, to tell his parents where he would be. Steve said he knew a nice restaurant a town away, where there would be very little chance of anyone from Arbella seeing them together. As Marcie went to the closet to pick out something to wear, she wondered how much more it would be possible to discreetly learn about Melissa's ghost in the next two and a half days. Already it was Friday and she had to leave by Sunday afternoon to be back at work on Monday. What was the likelihood of anything happening? She had drawn up a chart of the "ghost sightings" Steve had told her about. This showed that a week had gone by between the attack on Buster and Mrs. Watkins' spotting of the ghost in the supermarket parking lot. There was another week between that and Kyle Root being scared half to death outside the high school, then five days had passed before the attack on Penny Schuster on Wednesday. That made it unlikely that there would be another event until Monday at the earliest. Marcie shrugged as she pulled a dress out of the closet. Who knew whether vengeful ghosts kept to a timetable?

Marcie could tell by Steve's expression when she opened the door of his car that he was impressed by her appearance. Back in college, she had almost never worn anything other than jeans and a sweatshirt. She'd had lots of sweatshirts so it wouldn't get monotonous. It had even become a sort of collector thing with her—go somewhere and buy a commemorative sweatshirt. But after her first year at *Roaming New England,* she'd given almost all of them away to charity. Marcie thought of it as her caterpillar-into-a-butterfly move. She was getting on to the next stage of her life and happy to dump the unnecessary, concealing cocoon.

On the way out to the restaurant, Marcie told Steve about seeing Lisa having a rendezvous with a suspicious-looking man.

"I don't know this Lisa," Steve said. "She may not be a local. An old couple owns that motel, and as long as they get some money out of it they pretty much leave the running of it up to the person they hire as a manager." Steve paused. "I wasn't going to say anything. I figured it didn't matter because you were only going to be there a couple of days. But the place doesn't have the best reputation."

"Yeah, the sheets are kind of scratchy, the towels are threadbare, and the carpet looks like it was last replaced in the early sixties."

"I was thinking of something else."

"What?"

Steve blushed. "The police call it a hot bed rental."

"What does that mean?"

Steve blushed even redder. "Well . . . it's a place where prostitutes take their johns to . . . conduct business."

Marcie pictured the woman she had seen earlier wearing a rather obvious outfit, going into a room with a man. Marcie had noticed her in particular because she was a slender woman with long blond hair, rather like Melissa. Then Marcie remembered the suspicious look and the series of questions Lisa had given her when she found out that Marcie was a woman alone.

"My God! Steve, you didn't think I'd want to know that I was staying in a bordello?"

"It's not that bad. Lots of other people stay there. It's just that some of the rooms are used for that, and I know that it lacks some of the amenities."

"Oh, swell. So the odds are pretty good that mine wasn't used as a 'hot bed' last week. You know, somehow that doesn't make me feel a whole lot better. And as for lacking the amenities, not putting chocolates on my pillow when they turn down my bed is what I think of as lacking the amenities. This is what I call lacking the necessities."

"Sorry. But you did pick the place. I never would have put you there."

Marcie took a deep breath, then reached over to the steering wheel and squeezed Steve 's hand.

"You're absolutely right. I'm getting angry with you over something that's not your fault at all. I should be shouting at Sam, the cheap owner of the magazine who wants us to cut costs. Experience the local ambience my foot!" Marcie suddenly paused and smiled. "Maybe Amanda can use this example to get him to change the policy. He's an old-fashioned kind of guy who wouldn't want to be putting his female employees in any jeopardy."

"Can we get back to the subject of Lisa?" Steve asked.

"Sure."

"Aside from her odd behavior, do you have any other reason for connecting Lisa to Melissa's ghost?"

Marcie shrugged. "Only that Lisa's the right age, blond, and seems to be up to something suspicious. Otherwise I haven't discovered any connection."

Steve slowly cleared his throat and kept his eyes on the road.

"Do you think her behavior is significant enough that you should continue staying at the motel to investigate? I can suggest some other places."

Marcie frowned. "I hate situations where either choice stinks. I really don't want to stay in that dump, but I'm really curious as to what Lisa is up to."

Steve maintained a cautious silence.

"Oh, what the heck. I'll buy some new sheets and make up the bed. I can't exactly put in a new mattress, so that will have to do. At least it will lower the disgust factor a little bit. I'm not really worried about someone trying to pick me up. I doubt that anyone will think that I'm a hooker—my clothes aren't skimpy enough."

"Sounds like a good plan," Steve said.

"Do the police know that this is going on?"

"Sure."

"Then why don't they put a stop to it?"

"Oh, the police do a well-publicized raid on the place every few months. Then a few weeks later the business starts up again. Remember, the chief grew up here, so he's got a lot of friends, and some of them would probably like the place left open because they use the services. I imagine some money changes hands, and the police look the other way."

"Yeah, I suppose that sort of thing goes on everywhere."

"Aside from living in a moral sewer, how have you been enjoying your time in beautiful Arbella?" Steve asked.

Marcie grinned. "It's like a lot of small towns. There's not much for a tourist to do. But if you live here and become part of the community, I'm sure it could be a great place to live."

Steve gave a skeptical grunt.

"You know, it's not much different from where I live," Marcie continued, "except we're on the ocean, so we're geared a lot more to tourists. But in the winter there's even less to do than here. Most of the restaurants close, the fancier stores shut, and there's nothing bleaker than the beach on a dark, cold winter's day."

"I know, you're right. Arbella isn't really that bad when you look at it objectively. I guess everybody finds the town they grew up in to be confining."

"I lived in so many different locations, with my father in the military, that I never really had a hometown. To me it seems nice to have one place that holds all your memories of growing up."

"I see your point. But I think hometowns are more fun to return to for a visit, a place where you can show off all you've accomplished since you left. To keep living there when you get older is a little like staying too long at a party. No one is willing to tell you to leave, but everyone gets a bored look and yawns when they see you."

Marcie laughed at the image. "Yeah, I can see where that could happen. Too long in the same place with the same people can keep you from developing."

"Right. That's why I'm hoping this story will be my ticket out of here."

Marcie stared out the window at the trees and wondered how truthful to be. She decided she owed it to Steve to be honest even if it hurt him. A little hurt now would be better than a big disillusionment later.

"I don't want to sound discouraging, Steve, but a story in *Roaming New England* isn't going to open up a whole new career for you. We're not talking the *New Yorker* or *Vanity Fair.* It will be a nice addition to your résumé, but it isn't going to turn your life around."

Steve gave her a solemn nod. "I guess I know that. Even getting a piece in the *Globe* isn't going to turn my life around. But it seems like the best I can do right now, and I have to hope that every little bit will help."

They pulled into the parking lot of a restaurant named The Happy Cow. The sign showed a dancing cow with a maniacal grin.

"I hope you don't mind a steak place. They do have other things like chicken and pork on the menu."

"No problem," Marcie said, smiling at the irony of the sign. She doubted that any creature looked that happy at the thought of becoming an entrée.

The restaurant turned out to be a study in dark mahogany and weak indirect lighting. Seated in a room off the bar, they both had to hold their menus close to the candle on the table in order to read the offerings. Marcie chose a lamb chop, while Steve picked the smallest steak on the menu, which was described as "just right for the young cowpoke or the city dude watching his waistline."

"That's the only one I could find that wasn't enough meat for two," said Steve. "Too bad they make it sound so emasculating."

"People who run these places must feel that unless your plate is covered with meat, you won't come back. I find it intimidating to be confronted with all that food. You feel like it's your responsibility to see that none of it goes to waste."

"Maybe we can take the leftovers with us," Steve said.

"My motel room, despite its other charms, doesn't boast a refrigerator. But you can always take part of yours home."

"Not really. My mother doesn't like me putting things in the refrigerator."

"Couldn't you get a small refrigerator for your room?"

"I suppose. But that would seem like admitting that I'm going to be staying there for a long time."

"How long have you been there now?"

"Four years."

Marcie restrained herself from saying that was a long time.

"On your teacher's salary, couldn't you afford to rent a place?"

"Sure. But then I'd be admitting that I'm going to stay in teaching for a long time." Steve gave a deep sigh. "You see, it's one big vicious circle. Whatever I do, I'm making a commitment."

Their salads came, and Steve suggested that they talk about something less depressing than his life. He asked Marcie how her questioning of Penny Schuster had gone.

"Pretty good, if you want to hear the lie she's invented or that someone invented for her to cover up what happened." Marcie went on to tell Steve about the mysterious mugger.

"I wonder why she's going along with all this?" asked Steve.

"Probably because Brickmore has given her a sweetheart deal on the rent. Plus they are old friends."

"But isn't she afraid?"

Marcie paused. "You know, she didn't seem to be. Maybe she figured that the ghost was doing the rounds of the gang that went to the prom together and wouldn't be coming back to her. After all, there hasn't been a repeat attack on Buster. Or maybe she's more afraid of Brickmore than she is of a ghost, even one with a knife."

"You know, there's one really funny thing about these attacks."

"What's that?"

"No one has been hurt really bad. From what I know, Buster probably got the worst of it, and even he was out of the hospital by the next day. If I were a ghost out for revenge, I wouldn't limit my campaign of vengeance to a few minor cuts."

"When Penny was telling me what happened, I think she was describing it accurately except for substituting a mugger for the ghost. And at one point the attacker stumbled, and that allowed her to escape into the house."

"And Buster's ghost never followed him as he ran across the parking lot. I'm sure that if she'd been a little quicker, she probably could have finished him off," Steve said.

"So what's going on here?" Marcie asked. "Do we have a ghost who can't close the deal?"

"Or doesn't want to."

"Maybe she's only trying to get some publicity so an old case will be reopened."

"That will never happen as long as Grundfeld is in charge. He and Brickmore have kept a tight lid on this whole thing. As long as the injuries are relatively minor, only a few people are going to learn about it."

"But doesn't he have to report to the politicians, the mayor or city council? They won't be happy if Arbella becomes known as a place where you can see the sights and get attacked by a crazed ghost. They could force him to reopen the case."

"I'm sure the mayor and city council would step in if it got that bad."

"But so far Brickmore has managed to keep a lid on things. And you know what that means?"

"She either ups the ante or gives up."

They finished their salads, and their dinners arrived. After a few moments of quiet eating, Steve said, "You know how I promised that I wouldn't do any interviewing today?"

Marcie's eyes narrowed suspiciously. "Are you going to tell me that you didn't keep that promise?"

"Well, I just happened to find myself in the same faculty room as Kim Tyler."

"You just happened to find yourself there?"

"Yeah. Anyway, since we were alone in the same room, I thought I'd ask a few questions."

Marcie groaned. "You're just not taking this whole thing seriously enough, Steve. This Brickmore guy is a big shot in town, and he wants to keep this quiet, like in a tomb. The other night at the hospital he saw that you were involved. If he thinks you won't back off, something bad is going happen to you."

"But I need to talk to these people for the story."

"Maybe not. Maybe we've got enough to go with already. You know we don't have to be investigative reporters. We just need enough to write up a good ghost story. We've got descriptions of all the attacks. If any more happen, we can just plug them in later."

Steve shook his head. "I think this ghost story can blow wide open what happened to Melissa all those years ago.

If we keep pressing, I think we'll have more than just a good ghost story. We'll have solved a major crime."

Marcie sighed. "So what did you say to Tyler?"

"I let her know that I knew she had been friends with Melissa in high school. And I asked her if she was worried that she'd be the next one on the ghost's vengeance list."

"What good was that supposed to do?"

"I figured that maybe I could frighten her into telling me what happened on the night of the dance."

"The police already questioned everyone at the time."

"And they obviously didn't get honest answers, or the murder would have been solved."

"Only if someone at the prom killed her. We don't know that."

"But the ghost does or thinks she does. Right now that's good enough for me."

"Well, your attempt to frighten Tyler should get Brick more furious than ever."

Steve casually waved a hand to show none of that mattered to him and got some steak sauce on his shirt.

"Darn, I bet that's going to stain."

Marcie almost said that his mother could probably treat it with a stain remover, but decided that would be insulting. She figured no man wants to be talked to like a little boy even if he is living in his parents' basement. She was about to press her point that Steve shouldn't do anything further to get Brickmore angry when music began playing in Steve's coat pocket, and he pulled out his cell phone.

She heard him say hello to a Mrs. Maes. Then he said, "Who is it? Where is he? How's he doing?" Whatever answers he got, Marcie decided that he must have liked what he heard because he ended by saying, "We'll be right there."

He turned off his cell phone and looked across at Marcie, his eyes sparkling with excitement.

"There's been another attack. We've got to roll."

Steve turned around and began gesturing emphatically to their waitress. Marcie looked down at her almost full plate and pictured what a congealed mass it would be in a couple of hours, and decided that it wasn't worth taking it with her. She'd go out for a hamburger later if she were still hungry.

"In life there are few events worth missing dinner over" was one of her father's rare sayings that had proven true for Marcie. As she got up from the table, she looked back longingly at her meal, hoping the adage wasn't about to be proven true yet again.

Chapter Nine

"What's the matter with you?" Grundfeld asked. "You must go what, two hundred pounds, and you couldn't take the knife away from a little girl?"

James sat on the examining table. He was naked to the waist and there was a white dressing on the tops of his shoulders like epaulets of some unusual military rank. The doctor had just finished putting several stitches in each shoulder and told Kerr to wait there for a few minutes and he'd come back to give him further instructions.

"She wasn't a small girl, and the knife was very big. I'd like to see what you would have done under the same circumstances."

Grundfeld grunted derisively. "I doubt that I'm going to find out, because I'm not on the hit list. I wasn't in your cozy little group that night."

"You were at the prom."

"So were lots of other people, but the ghost only seems

interested in the five of you. Maybe after she's gone through her list once, she'll start over again, and this time she'll finish the job."

James opened his mouth to respond, but the door opened and he thought better of it. Roger Brickmore came into the room carrying a piece of paper that he handed to James.

"The doctor said you could leave. Just follow these directions for the next few days and you'll be fine."

"Yeah, I'll be fine unless she comes back again."

"Who said that will happen?"

James looked over at Grundfeld.

"Charlie, could you let good sense govern your mouth for a change?" Brickmore said, staring hard at the chief.

Grundfeld grinned. "I was just kidding. The guy can't take a joke."

Brick gave a disgusted shake of his head. "You don't know how hard a time I had convincing Penny that she doesn't need around-the-clock police protection, because the ghost is going to go through all five of us first."

"Convincing Penny of anything isn't so hard," Grundfeld said with a leering smile. "Even back in school, Penny's mind wasn't the thing that developed most."

"She's smart enough to be afraid," Brick snapped. "Even Buster came around asking for protection. I've got one of our plainclothes security guards from the plant hanging out with him every night at the club."

"At least he's got somebody sober to drive him home," the chief said. "That alone should increase his chances of survival."

"This isn't funny," James said, pulling on his shirt and wincing as he raised his arm. "You may think this is all a big gag, Charlie, but what if this person is serious and does plan to kill each of us in some macabre way? Maybe all we've seen is her warm-up."

Grundfeld shook his head. "If she wanted to do that, then you, Buster, and Penny would already be dead. Serial killers don't do warm-ups on the people they plan to kill. If she's practicing on Buster, Penny, and you, then she has somebody else in mind for the big show."

"So now you're a profiler who knows the minds of serial killers."

"I know more about it than some guy who spends all his time playing with dogs and cats."

"This isn't getting us anywhere," Brick said. He turned to Grundfeld. "Can you spare someone to keep an eye on James until we've caught this lunatic?"

"It'll be hard to find a good man that I can spare, but I guess I can find someone to cover his butt for part of the day."

"I also got a call from Kim Tyler today," Brick said. "Steve Rostow got her all upset by suggesting that she is probably the ghost's next victim."

Grundfeld shrugged. "She probably is."

"Well, get someone on her too. And if Rostow keeps causing trouble, we may have to think of a way to discourage his interest."

"That's something I'd like to do," the chief said.

Brick turned to James, who was all dressed and shifting from foot to foot, as though anxious to leave the hospital. "Was there anything familiar about her? Could she have been someone you know?"

He shrugged helplessly. "She could have been anyone. With all that blood and the knife, I didn't focus on her face."

"I understand, James," Brick said, gently patting him on the back. "And don't worry. Charlie and I are going to take care of you." He glanced over his shoulder at the chief, who gave a reluctant nod.

"Why is someone doing this?" James asked. "Is it a serial killer?"

"She hasn't killed anyone yet," Brick reminded him. "Just between the three of us, I think the whole thing is political."

"Political?" Kerr asked.

Brick looked at his hands as if he were a humble laborer. "It's not exactly common knowledge, but there's been some talk in Hartford about my being a candidate for national political office. I think someone is trying to knock me out of contention by bringing up this whole Melissa Harrison mess. So far I've convinced the local paper to leave out the garish details that would link these events to Melissa's murder, but we've got to stop this soon or else it's bound to leak out."

"Susan at the restaurant told me that there was a young woman in her place the other day asking about Melissa Harrison. Of course, Susan didn't say much, but she figured she'd better tell me about it anyway," Grundfeld said and winked. "Susan knows that I'd have the Board of Health swarming over that place in a heartbeat if I found she was holding out on me."

"Susan runs a clean place," Kerr said.

"We'd find something. We *always* find something."

"Did she have any more information on this young woman?" asked Brick.

"Only that she worked for some magazine."

Brick ran a hand though his thick hair. "National or even

regional coverage, that's exactly what I don't need. Do you have any idea who she is?" he asked Grundfeld.

The chief shook his head. "But she has to be staying somewhere, probably at one of those big motels out near the highway. I'll check around. She shouldn't be too hard to find."

"So are you saying that this is all a political thing, and the ghost doesn't really plan to kill anyone to avenge Melissa?" asked James.

"I think she just wants to get enough publicity to have the state police decide to reopen the Harrison case. If that happened, the party would drop me like a hot potato," said Brick.

"So I don't have to worry about being attacked again?" James asked Brick. "This is some actress who's been hired to attack people in order to sidetrack your political career? It's hard to believe that anyone in government would hire someone to go around stabbing people."

"Don't be naive, James," Brickmore said. "They've employed people to do a lot worse."

"Just keep your mouth shut, and you'll come out of this smelling like a rose," Grundfeld said.

He opened the door for Brickmore, then went through it himself, brushing past James and giving him a contemptuous look.

Chapter Ten

"Here we are," Steve announced. "We're at the hospital."

Having seen the signs and the large building, Marcie didn't think the announcement was necessary. Steve swung the car into the driveway marked for the emergency room and pulled into a space in the parking lot. He opened the door and jumped out.

"I'm going to find out from Mrs. Maes if they're still here," he called over his shoulder.

"Hold it a minute." Steve stood still long enough for Marcie to catch up. "I think it would be best if I remained out of sight. That way I might be able to secretly interview our other victims, like I did with Penny."

"Fine. Meet me back at the car when it's all over. They'll be coming out of that door," Steve said, pointing to "sliding doors with EMERGENCY ROOM written over the top. "I'm going to see if I can find Mrs. Maes."

After Steve left, Marcie, staying in the shadows, walked closer to the emergency room door, trying to find a place where she could hide and still have an unobstructed view of anyone coming out. Finally, she found a place at the corner of the building where a large bush would pretty much hide her, yet she could easily peek around it to see anyone leaving the emergency room. Marcie wasn't sure that there was any point to this. James Kerr wasn't likely to give Steve an interview, and there was a good chance that Grundfeld and Brick would be there. Marcie was sure that if Steve kept up the pressure on them, they'd eventually do something drastic.

"Still on the team with Steve?" a voice behind her asked.

Marcie gave a soft yelp of surprise and turned around to see Jena Conway in uniform standing a few feet behind her.

"You scared the wits out of me," Marcie said.

"Sorry. But if you're going to go lurking around spying on people, you'd better keep your ears open."

"Why are you here?"

"I drove the chief over. He told me to wait with the car, but I got bored and decided to take a little walk. Then I spotted you doing your Indian scout impersonation, and I'm afraid I couldn't resist."

"Do you know why the chief is here?"

"Yeah. The same reason you and Steve are. James Kerr was attacked. I was just about ready to go off duty when the chief grabbed me to bring him over here. I pulled into the parking lot right behind Brick."

"I've been meaning to ask you, why does the chief need a driver?" Marcie asked.

Jena shrugged. "I guess it's some kind of status thing. I don't take him everywhere; sometimes he goes off by himself."

"What do you think they're up to in there?"

"Oh, I can make a pretty good guess at that. I expect the three of them are trying to put a lid on this ghost business, so it doesn't get a lot of publicity. That would be very bad, for Mr. Brickmore in particular."

"Why? I mean aside from the fact that he doesn't want people to know that he was once suspected of being a murderer."

"From what I've heard around town, he'd like to be the next senator from our great state. And it wouldn't help his chances if there's new publicity that he was once a murder suspect."

"But it's not like he was ever tried for it. There must have been other suspects."

"I suppose there were, but from what I've heard from the old-timers at the station, he was the leading contender. A lot of people in town think that if he'd been anyone other than a Brickmore, the police would have tried a lot harder to get an indictment."

"So who do you think is going around town playing at being a ghost?" Marcie asked.

"Beats me. But eventually they're going to get caught. There are only two people left on the list who haven't been attacked, so all we have to do is keep a close eye on the two of them, and eventually the ghost will come to us."

"So you'll use Kimberly Tyler and Roger Brickmore as bait?"

"That's an ugly but accurate way to put it. We'll actually be guarding them, but with unmarked cars. That way the ghost won't know we're there and will come out in the open to strike."

"Was that Chief Grundfeld's idea? Sounds pretty sophisticated, given what I've heard about him."

"Don't underestimate the chief. He may like to use his hands, but he can use his head as well."

Marcie watched as Steve hurried out the emergency room door and took up a position along the edge of the sidewalk, his reporter's notebook at the ready. A minute later, three men came out of the building.

Jena whispered in her ear, "The guy in the lead is Roger Brickmore. The fellow in the middle must be James Kerr, because I don't recognize him, and that's Chief Grundfeld bringing up the rear."

From what she had heard, Marcie had formed a mental picture of Brick as a large, loutish man whose appearance would be intimidating, but in reality he was a slender, handsome man who looked more like a news anchor than a thug. Grundfeld, however, did look the part. His bald head pushed forward aggressively as if he were perpetually angry and just waiting for an opportunity to let the anger out. When Steve stepped forward and asked Kerr for an opportunity to speak with him, that was just the opportunity Grundfeld was waiting for. He stepped forward and pushed Steve hard enough for him to fall to the ground. While Jena sprinted past Marcie, Grundfeld kicked Steve, but he had curled up into a ball, taking the kick on his arms. The chief was looking to take another shot and had brought his foot back ready to do so, when Jena rushed past him and virtually threw herself on top of Steve.

She looked over her shoulder at Grundfeld and said, "I'll cuff him, chief, and take him downtown."

"Don't bother," Grundfeld said a moment later, when he had calmed down. He probably figured he didn't have a case, especially since a couple of nurses from the emergency room were standing outside looking on in shock and could serve as witnesses.

Grundfeld waited until Steve had regained his feet, then stuck his face close to his and said, "Rostow, if you give me any reason to believe that you've told anyone about this crime, I'll see that your ass ends up in jail. And I don't mean just for one night. And when you do get out, you'll have no job to return to, and you'll never live happily in this town again. Do you understand me?"

"I understand," Steve said in a remarkably clear voice, considering the circumstances.

"Make sure you do," the chief said, poking him hard four times in the chest with his index finger to emphasize each word. Then he smiled contemptuously. "Not that the *Arbella Archives* would ever publish anything you wrote about this, boy reporter."

Marcie could see Steve's hands clench into fists at his side.

The chief jerked his head toward Jena, indicating that she should bring his car around, and she hurried on ahead of him. Brickmore and Kerr were already in their cars waiting to leave the parking lot. Grundfeld stopped by the open driver's windows of each of them and said something.

Marcie walked down to the sidewalk.

"Are you okay?" she asked Steve.

"Yeah. I'll probably have a bruise on the shoulder where he kicked me. I guess I should count myself lucky that he didn't hit my head or get a kidney."

"He was way out of line. Somebody should arrest him," said Mrs. Maes. She and the other nurse stood there shaking their heads.

"Maybe you'd better let us take you inside and check to be sure you're all right."

"Thanks, but I'm fine, Mrs. Maes," Steve said.

"This is Nurse Thompson," Mrs. Maes said, turning to the woman next to her. "She heard most of what the injured man said to the other two."

Nurse Thompson nodded. "The chief very rudely told me to leave the room even though I always stay to assist the doctor, and the doctor didn't stand up for me. So I went into the linen closet next door. It has an open vent into the treatment room. You can hear things just like you were there in the room."

"What did you hear?" Steve asked, picking his spiral notebook off the ground where it had fallen when he was attacked.

"You won't tell anyone that I told you all this, will you?"

"You will only be referred to as a reliable source."

Nurse Thompson smiled as if she sort of liked the new title. "Well, they didn't say much about what had happened while the doctor was in the room. The chief didn't let Mr. Kerr speak. He just kept saying to the doctor that it was a mugging."

"What about Brickmore?"

"He didn't say anything until the doctor left the room, but then he asked Mr. Kerr to tell him exactly what happened."

"Which was?" Steve asked.

While Nurse Thompson recounted the attack by the ghost on James, Steve scribbled furiously in his notebook.

"Did they seem to take what he was saying seriously?" asked Marcie.

"Very seriously. Nobody was telling him to cut it out

and stop telling stories or anything like that. They seemed to believe that there really was someone attacking the people who went to the prom with Mr. Brickmore."

"And Brick was worried about what the publicity would do to his political chances," said Marcie.

"He sure was. That seemed to be the thing that bothered him the most."

Marcie and Steve thanked the nurse for her information and walked back to the car. Steve groaned a bit as he slid behind the wheel.

"What's the matter?" Marcie asked.

"My arm hurts a little more than I thought it would."

"Maybe you should get an X-ray."

"It'll be fine. Maybe I should have gotten up and hit him back rather than curling up on the ground like some weakling," he said, starting the engine.

"Steve, it would only have gotten you arrested. And you'd have given Grundfeld an excuse to hurt you even more. He must outweigh you by seventy-five pounds."

"But most of it's fat."

Marcie laughed. "Still, it was a good thing you didn't try to find out, and you owe Jena some thanks for intervening."

"Yeah, I guess I do. Jena was smart and pretty brave to come between me and the chief like that."

"She sure was," Marcie said, and was surprised to find that she was suddenly jealous of her. She decided to change the subject. "So, what do we do next? We've heard at least a secondhand version of what happened to each of the people who were attacked, and I'm not sure that puts us much further ahead. We still have no idea who's going around town pretending to be Melissa's ghost."

"And we don't know why," Steve added. "Brickmore

apparently thinks it's someone who wants to ruin his budding political career."

Marcie shook her head. "Running around town pretending to be a ghost and knifing people seems way too bizarre and complicated for someone with only a political motive. Plus there haven't been any headlines because Grundfeld and Brickmore have kept a tight lid on the whole thing. You're the only one who's any threat to them."

"Okay, if it isn't somebody looking to ruin Brickmore's political career, what is the ghost up to?"

"Revenge."

"Do you really think so?"

"Isn't that the way it works in all those horror movies? The ghost comes back to get revenge for what happened while it was still alive."

"Right. But let's stay in touch with reality here, Marcie. There isn't really a ghost."

"Okay. But the person who is pretending to be the ghost is trying to frighten people by preying on their guilty consciences. No one is being killed, but I think the attacker is hoping that someone will break and go to the police with the true story of what happened that night."

"You're assuming that they know what happened, that one of them is guilty."

"I'm just saying that's what the ghost believes."

"And what if none of them go to the police?" Steve asked.

Marcie looked out the window at the dark streets going by.

"Then I think the ghost might just decide to take revenge for herself."

Steve pulled into the motel parking lot.

"So maybe we should be looking into the past to find out who would care enough about Melissa to start taking revenge, and why they'd wait so long."

"It's been exactly twenty years since her death. Maybe the ghost has a sense of history. What about Melissa's family? Are any of them still around?"

"Her mother."

"She might be feeling pretty vengeful."

"Like I told you, the parents felt pretty guilty for not being home that night when Melissa called. But I'm not sure I see her mother being able to convincingly imitate a high school girl."

"Did she have any other family?"

"A younger brother. I have no idea what happened to him." Steve paused and gave Marcie a surprised look. "You don't think it could be her brother in drag attacking these people?"

"Sounds like a Hitchcock movie. I kind of doubt it. He'd be in his mid- to late thirties by now. No one seems to have any doubts that it was a woman who attacked them."

"But it was dark, and they were under stress."

"Let's not go down that road until we have to," said Marcie. She looked around at the dark parking lot and felt a shiver down her spine. "Look, maybe we'd better not sit out here in the open if we're trying to avoid having the chief link us together."

"We could go in your room and talk."

Marcie shook her head. "No offense, but I don't want to get arrested for solicitation, even accidentally. This could be the night that Grundfeld decides to launch one of his raids."

"Good point. Tomorrow is Saturday. Why don't we meet for breakfast outside of town? I'll swing by here at eight thirty and you can follow me in your car."

"Sounds fine," Marcie said.

As she walked to the door of her motel room, she wondered exactly what purpose it would serve to get together to rehash the few facts they had. It might be better if she urged Steve to just write the story with the information he had now and submit it, because it sure didn't look as though they were learning much by talking to the people in Arbella. Before going into her room, Marcie decided to buy a soda from the machine around the corner from the office. As she rounded the corner, she saw the blond woman she had spotted that morning going into her room with a man. Her tight-fitting dress had been replaced with an equally tight pair of shorts and a tank top.

The woman looked up as Marcie approached. "Do you have change for a dollar bill? This machine won't take paper money."

Marcie reached in her pocket and found four quarters.

"Thanks. Are you staying here too?" she asked.

"Sort of," Marcie replied. "I'll be leaving soon."

"Yeah, I know what you mean. I only stay here from Thursdays until Sundays; then I head right back home to my two little girls. Do you have any children?"

Marcie shook her head.

"I don't know if I'd be able to keep on doing this if I didn't have the girls."

Marcie decided that it was time to see if she could find out more about Lisa.

"What's the story with the blond who works in the office?" she asked.

"What do you mean?" The smile disappeared from her face, replaced by wariness.

"I keep seeing her running off into the woods to meet some guy."

The woman quickly shoved her change into the machine and pulled out her cola.

"I don't get involved in stuff like that." She turned to Marcie, and her face softened. "You shouldn't either. You'll learn that in this business asking questions is dangerous."

Chapter Eleven

Kim Tyler stood in the center of her living room, which had always made her feel comfortable and secure, and instead felt nervous and exposed. She went to the front window and peeked around the side of the shade. Yes, the unmarked patrol car was still under the tree three houses down. Larry Peters, the officer in the car, was there to keep her safe. The fact that she'd had Larry in class a mere four years ago didn't fill Kim with confidence. No matter how alert and competent he might be, she still felt as if a child were guarding her.

To give him his due, Larry had gone through the house carefully when he'd arrived a half hour ago. He'd checked every room and all the doors and windows, even going down in the cellar. Although Kim kept telling herself that she was safer right now with a personal armed guard than she had been on any other night in her life, her emotions refused to listen to reason. On some level, Kim wished that she had never called Penny to find out what had happened to her.

She and Penny had been pretty close during high school through their friendship with Brick, but in reality they'd had little in common. Penny was the cheerleader type, pretty, vivacious, but with no long-range goals beyond landing a handsome husband and settling down in Arbella. Kim had hoped for more. She'd wanted to be a teacher, figuring that would enable her to move somewhere else and leave her hometown behind. But she had graduated from college during a slow economic period, and Brick's offer to help her get a job at the high school had been too tempting. She had gone through a brief but bad marriage and now lived on her own. Not so different from Penny, she thought sadly.

Deciding that she had more in common with Penny than she cared to admit and prodded by Steve Rostow's remarks in the faculty room that afternoon, Kim had given her a call to see how she was after the mugging and to find out the truth about the episode. At first, Penny had said nothing beyond what was in the newspaper. Kim relaxed and let the conversation move on to reminiscences about high school. Just as she was about to hang up, Penny, perhaps motivated by recollections of their past friendship, poured out in great detail what had really happened. Although Penny had never shown language skills beyond the bare minimum, she had managed to describe the attack with a vividness that made Kim's blood run cold.

Kim had sat with a trembling hand clenched around the phone receiver, hardly believing what she was hearing. Hanging up without saying good-bye, she had called Buster, and, after feeble resistance, had learned that something similar had happened to him.

Her next call had been to Brick. Although she had always

been a little afraid of him because of his power in the town and tendency to be manipulative, this time her fear and anger motivated her to tear into him for not notifying her of what was going on and not offering her police protection.

Brick had tried to downplay the danger, but he promised to discuss the matter with Charlie Grundfeld. Chief Grundfeld, a man she'd never had anything but contempt for, had tagged along on the edges of their group in high school, never being fully accepted. But later that evening, Brick had called her back, told her about the attack on James Kerr, and guaranteed her police protection starting immediately.

Kim quickly guessed, when she saw they were using unmarked cars, that they were setting a trap for the ghost. Larry had even admitted that there would be two more patrol cars less than a mile away all night in case he needed backup—clearly a trap, with her as the bait. Brick was probably at an undisclosed location surrounded by armed guards, thought Kim, while she was like a staked-out goat waiting for the tiger. She paced up and down the living room, wondering how many days she could put up with this tension.

Suddenly, she heard something. She stopped pacing. It had come from right under where she was standing. Kim rocked back and forth on her feet to see if it had been the squeaking of a loose board, but was unable to duplicate the sound. Standing very still, she listened. For the longest time there was nothing, then just as she was about to resume pacing she heard it—the sound of something being moved in the basement. She'd had lots of things stored there since her parents sold their home in the north and moved to Florida. It would be difficult for anyone to walk around without bumping into something. Again she spent a long minute listening, but this time she heard nothing.

Kim decided that she didn't need to hear a marching band before being concerned. This was something that needed to be checked out, and not by her. Larry had told her that if she wanted him to come to her assistance, she should blink the front lights twice. She did that, and watched out the window as Larry immediately came trotting across the street.

"What's up?" Larry asked when she let him into the living room.

"I thought I heard something in the basement," Kim said, realizing as she said it out loud that she sounded a lot like a child worrying about the bogeyman under the bed.

"I checked down there," Larry said doubtfully. Seeing the look on her face, he quickly added, "Although it never hurts to check twice."

Turning on the light for the cellar stairs, Larry proceeded down with his gun drawn. Kim remained by the front door, ready to run for a neighbor's house at the first sound of trouble.

She heard Larry's voice but was too far away to catch what he was saying. Against her better judgment, she took a couple of steps closer to the open cellar door.

"Come here," she heard Larry say. "Come here, you."

Kim thought that Larry must be very brave to talk to a ghost with a knife as if it were a misbehaving child.

"Come here! Now!" Larry ordered.

There was the sound of a struggle, and Kim moved closer to her front door.

"Ouch!" Larry said loud enough for her to hear. "You didn't have to do that."

Kim's hand went to the door handle, ready to turn it and bolt. Then she heard slow, heavy footsteps coming up the stairs. She wasn't sure what to do. Should she run before seeing who it was? Although sorely tempted to run, Kim was aware how silly she would look if it turned out to be nothing. Finally she decided to open the door and stand in the doorway ready to run. Poised like this, she waited as the footsteps approached.

Finally Larry appeared at the top of the steps. His hair was mussed and he was sucking on his left thumb. In his arms he was carrying something.

"It was just your cat. I guess we accidentally locked it in the basement. The darn thing bit me when I tried to pick it up," he said in an aggrieved tone, as if she should have warned him that she possessed a dangerous creature.

Kim stared at him with her mouth open. Larry put the cat down and it quickly ran across the room, darted between her legs, and shot out the door.

"Great," Larry said in disgust. "I hope your cat knows enough to come home, because I can't be chasing it around the neighborhood."

Kim stopped staring and shook her head.

"I don't have a cat," she said.

Chapter Twelve

The next morning, Marcie got up early to run before having breakfast with Steve.

She'd had a good night's sleep because Steve had stopped at a small shopping mall and purchased new sheets that she had immediately put on her bed. She now took the road in the direction that led out of town. The morning was cool, but by the time she had run half a mile, Marcie was glad that she hadn't worn more than a T-shirt and running shorts, because there was little breeze and the sun was warm. When she guessed that she had probably gone a mile, Marcie turned around and ran back, trying to pick up her speed. As she neared the motel, she saw a police car parked in front of the office. Wondering if Grundfeld had found out her whereabouts, she ran past the motel, then came back on the other side of the street and took cover behind a tree that allowed her to watch the office door.

After five minutes, she started to shiver as the sweat began to dry. She rubbed her arms and legs to increase circulation, hoping that whoever was in the office would come out soon. She didn't have long to wait, because about five minutes later the door opened and Grundfeld strolled out. Right behind him was Lisa. For a moment, Marcie thought that he was heading for her room, but instead he went to the patrol car and opened the door. He stood there for a moment, leaning on the door and talking to Lisa, who came over and stood quite close to him, as if they wanted to keep their conversation confidential. A minute later he nodded, got in the car, closed the door, and after leaning out the window to have one last word with Lisa, sped out of the parking lot, scattering the gravel.

Marcie waited another minute or two, then ran across the street as if she had just come back from her run.

She headed straight for her room, but before she could open the door, Lisa came out of the office and called to her, "Did you have a good run?"

"Fine," Marcie said, putting her key in the door lock.

"Hang on, I want to talk to you for a moment," Lisa said.

Lisa came close to her and spoke in a soft voice. "Look, I don't know if you realize, but this motel doesn't have the greatest reputation."

Marcie nodded. "So I've heard."

"I know you aren't part of that clientele, so maybe it would be better if you went somewhere that would be more pleasant for you." Lisa's voice came close to making that a demand rather than a request.

"Tonight's my last night. I'm going home tomorrow."

Lisa nodded. "Sometimes things happen here at night. So if you should hear any loud noises, like people fighting, keep your door closed and don't pay any attention. Know what I mean?"

"Yeah," Marcie snapped, put off by being bossed around.

Lisa shrugged. "I'm only telling you this for your own good."

"Right."

Marcie went into her room and closed the door. She stood there for a moment trying to figure out what the connection might be between Lisa and Grundfeld and between Lisa and the man in the woods. Also, could there be any possible connection between all of this and the ghost of Melissa Harrison? Put a bloody prom dress on Lisa and she would fit the general description of the ghost, but so would lots of other young women. Marcie took off her running outfit and headed for the bathroom. A shower would make her feel better, even if it wouldn't provide answers to her questions.

Promptly at eight thirty, Steve pulled into the parking lot of the motel. Marcie was already in her car. She waved out the window, then followed him out to the road. She wished that they'd agreed to meet at the restaurant rather than at the motel. Lisa was probably at the window taking down Steve's license plate number at this very moment. They turned left and went out of town along her running route, but they kept going for about three more miles until they pulled into the parking lot of a small restaurant.

"The food here is good, and it's across the town line, so I don't think we'll run into Grundfeld," Steve said as they walked toward the restaurant door.

"I've already had that pleasure today," Marcie said. Steve gave her a startled look. "I'll explain once we're inside."

After they were seated and had placed their order, Marcie told Steve what had happened.

"I wonder why Grundfeld was there?" Steve wondered.

"Maybe he was scheduling his next phony raid."

"I doubt he'd do that in person. There must be something more important going on."

"Like what?"

Steve shrugged. "Who knows what Grundfeld might be up to?"

"You know, I was wondering if Lisa could be our ghost. And maybe Grundfeld and the guy in the woods are somehow the ringleaders of the whole thing."

"Why would they do that?"

Marcie shrugged. "Maybe Grundfeld is tired of playing second fiddle to Brick. If he could get this case reopened, the chief might figure that he could get a conviction and be the one running this town."

"From what I can find, there isn't enough evidence to prove that Brick killed Melissa, so I don't see how reopening the case will help. Plus, if this becomes big enough, the state police might get involved, and I don't think Grundfeld would like the state boys poking around in his territory."

"Okay, so we forget about Grundfeld. Where does that leave us?"

The waitress arrived with their orders, Marcie getting one egg over easy with toast, while Steve had two eggs on top of a mountain of hash. Marcie looked at his breakfast and his skinny frame and knew that sometimes nature just wasn't fair.

"I think you were on the right track last night," Steve said once the waitress had left. "This has to be somebody from the past."

"This ghost apparently looks young. I doubt that she was around forty years ago."

"Well, maybe she has some link to the past, even if she wasn't alive then."

"How are we going to find out what was going on twenty years ago at Arbella High?" Marcie asked, wiping up egg yoke with a piece of toast.

Steve's eyes sparkled. "Exactly the question I asked myself after I dropped you off last night. Then the answer came to me: Lois Pritchard."

"Okay, I'll bite. Who's Lois Pritchard?"

"A former English teacher at Arbella who retired last year after thirty years of service."

"So she would have been around when Brick and his buddies were students. But are you sure she knew them?"

"That's why I gave her a call last night to find out."

"And?" Marcie asked.

"Well, not a complete success, but not bad. She had Brick, Kim, and James in her honors English class. She knew Buster, largely from his football highlights and the times when she supervised detention. Penny she remembered less well—couldn't put a face to the name."

"That's still pretty good. Could she tell you anything about them?"

"Before I could ask, she invited me over to visit this morning. I got to know her pretty well during the last couple of years before she retired, and we always got along. I asked her if I could bring you along, and she agreed."

"What time?"

Steve checked his watch. "We've got about ten minutes to finish up here and vamoose. She wanted us there by nine because she's got a ten o'clock tee time at the country club."

"I'll bet she doesn't fit the standard image of a retired spinster schoolteacher."

"She's no spinster; she's divorced. But you're right—there isn't much of the lace doilies and lily of the valley about her."

"Hmm. I just hope we can find out some useful information that will relate to the situation today."

"There's a good chance. Lois told me there was one other person in that same honors class who was involved in this whole thing."

"Who?"

"Melissa Harrison, the victim."

Although Marcie could hardly believe it, Steve managed to finish his eggs and a mountain of hash in less than ten minutes. It hadn't been pretty to watch, but he had gotten the job done. So they were pulling up in front of Lois Pritchard's house right on time. The small Cape Cod–style house was on a corner lot with carefully arranged plantings along the front walk. All in all, it appeared to be a place that was well tended.

They rang the bell and the door was opened by a woman in her sixties wearing shorts and a polo shirt. "Glad you got here on time so we'll have a chance to talk," she said, motioning for them both to come inside. She shook Marcie's hand and gave Steve a hug.

"Your plantings are wonderful," Marcie said.

"Yes, aren't they?" the woman agreed. "I have a man who takes care of all that for me. I can't be bothered with gardening. That's for old people."

They were directed into the front room on the right, which turned out to be a small but nicely decorated living room. Marcie refrained from commenting on the décor, assuming a professional had probably done that as well. Mrs. Pritchard offered them coffee, but warned that it would be instant because she never bothered with it herself. Marcie and Steve both declined, saying they had just had breakfast.

The woman settled back in an upholstered chair and looked at them shrewdly. "So, you're interested in Brick and his group of friends back when they were in high school. Why are you looking into that now?"

On the way over, Steve and Marcie had discussed how they might answer this question and agreed they had to tell Lois Pritchard the truth. So Steve gave her a quick but complete summary of the events regarding Melissa's ghost. When they were done, Mrs. Prichard, who had let them talk without asking a question or making a comment, gave a deep sigh.

"I always had a feeling that Melissa's murder would raise its ugly head again. I didn't imagine it would be done as dramatically as this, but I thought that this was a crime committed by a local person, and crimes like that have a way of coming home to roost."

"You didn't go along with the traveling-serial-killer idea?" asked Marcie.

The woman shook her head. "Melissa left that dance early for a reason. I mean, who rushes off from their senior prom? I've always thought that whatever got her that upset must be involved in her murder."

"What kind of a girl was Melissa?" asked Marcie.

"She was very pretty, with long blond hair, quite tall and slender. She probably could have gone out for cheerleading, but she preferred to get involved with the school's tutoring program. She was a good student, but not especially intelligent. I would have described her as nice rather than smart. She believed in helping people. She told me once that she wanted to go to college to study social work. I don't know if I've ever known another student as attractive as she who was less aware of her own beauty."

"How did she ever get involved with Brick?" Steve asked.

The woman thought for a moment. "All I can remember is that right after New Year's I noticed that Roger Brickmore was hanging around her before class. At first, I think Melissa just found it an annoyance. She was a sensible girl and had heard all the rumors about Roger. I could see that she wasn't laughing at his jokes or hanging all over him like some of the girls who were impressed by his money."

"Why did a family with that much money send their son to public school?" asked Marcie.

"Roger's father had a thing about not letting the family forget where they came from. His father had sent him to public school, so he thought it was good enough for his son. He believed that the only way to maintain the strong connection between Arbella and his family was by having his children grow up knowing the children from the town."

"And it worked," said Steve. "He's given jobs to lots of his friends, starting with Buster and Chief Grundfeld."

"Yes. That was the bad side of Mr. Brickmore's plan. Roger went through school like a little prince who was surrounded by servile attendants who hoped to gain in some way from his money and influence. He would have been better off attending a private school where all the students came from wealthy backgrounds. It would have been more egalitarian."

"Can we go back to Melissa?" Marcie asked. "Why did she change her mind about Brick?"

"To be honest, I can't be certain why she began to see him differently. I think it was because he did seem to actually change in his senior year. The arrogance and tendency to lord it over some of the other students disappeared. He'd always been a very capable student, but he never made much genuine effort in class. He affected a sort of rebellious attitude while at the same time he managed to get good grades. As a senior, however, he suddenly became much more involved with class discussions and even took seriously the opinions of other students."

"Why did he change?" asked Steve.

"I always suspected that his father had a long talk with him about his future. Maybe he told Roger that he'd have to take college more seriously or else he wouldn't pay for it. Roger's father was a very strict man about certain things, and I believe that Roger was really frightened of him."

"So Brick changed and began going out with Melissa. Did she become part of his gang?"

Mrs. Pritchard shook her head. "No. Roger continued to hang out with Buster, Penny, James, and Kimberly. But I don't think I ever saw Melissa with Roger and the gang. It was almost as if he had two lives going on simultaneously: his old life with the gang, and his new life with Melissa."

"Who was Roger involved with before Melissa?" asked Marcie.

Mrs. Pritchard shrugged. "You have to remember that I only saw him while he was in class and occasionally out in the hall or at a sports event. So I don't know very much about his social life. I had Roger as a student during his junior year as well, and I'd say that year he went from girl to girl. I frequently saw him walking down the hall holding hands with a pretty girl or kissing in the hall. But he went through a number of different pretty girls. But like I said, something changed at the beginning of his senior year."

"So the change in his senior year wasn't only in his attitude toward academics?" asked Steve.

"No. It was even a change in his attitude toward girls. He didn't seem as flirtatious, and I didn't see him out in the hall with a different girl each month. In fact, during that whole time I believe I only saw him genuinely interested in one girl before Melissa."

"Who was that?" asked Marcie.

"Rachel Carpenter. She was in the same English class as Roger, Melissa, Kimberly, and James Kerr."

"What do you know about her?" asked Steve.

"She was very pretty, but quite shy. She'd moved to Arbella over the summer before her senior year, so no one knew anything about her. Rachel was an excellent student, but very serious. You would almost think that she was from another country because she always seemed to be trying to figure out how to behave."

"What about her family?"

"She lived with her mother, who I believe was a recent widow. She got a job working at the Brickmore mill. I didn't know anything about the family except for the fact that they attended a small church right outside of town. I only know that because one of my students was a member and told me Rachel went there too."

"What type of church was it?"

"I'm not sure, but I think it was quite conservative. The one or two times I met Rachel's mother she impressed me as being very strict as well. I don't think Rachel was allowed to socialize with the other students. I asked her once if she was going to the girls' basketball game, and she said that her mother didn't approve of her going to that kind of thing. I asked her why not. All she said was that her mother thought the other children might be a bad influence."

"So she was a shy, unsophisticated but pretty girl," said Marcie. "How did she get involved with Roger Brickmore?"

"They sat across from each other in class. Otherwise, I have no idea. Like I said, I only saw them walking in the hall together. That caught my eye, because they seemed so ill suited to each other. I don't know what their relationship was like. I can't imagine Rachel's mother allowing her to date anyone, let alone Roger Brickmore."

"But their relationship didn't last into the second semester. Brick took up with Melissa then," said Steve.

"Yes, but it didn't exactly happen that way," Mrs. Pritchard said. "Rachel left school over the holidays and didn't come back. Her mother called the principal and told him that Rachel was going to be moving to Maine to live with her aunt, her mother's older sister. Apparently she'd had a heart attack and needed someone to take care of the housework for her. Presumably Rachel would live up there and finish out her time in high school."

"Why do you say 'presumably'?" asked Marcie.

"Well, I asked the school secretary if there had been any request for Rachel's records by another school system, and she said there hadn't."

"Maybe she waited until the next year," said Steve.

Mrs. Pritchard shook her head. "I got kind of interested in the whole thing and checked for the next two years—nothing. I even called Mrs. Carpenter to ask her if her daughter planned to finish school. She was very snippy with me and said that Rachel would return to school when she was able to and that it was no business of mine. I was so mad it even crossed my mind to call child welfare, but by then Rachel would have been nineteen."

"None of the other students knew anything about what happened to her?" asked Steve.

"Well, I didn't go around grilling them all to find out. But I did ask around discreetly, and no one seemed to have any idea. Rachel was such a quiet girl, with so few friends, that I doubt most people noticed she was gone."

"Is there anyone in town who would have any more information about all this?" asked Marcie.

"Her mother passed away five years ago. The only person I can think of is Reverend Carstairs. He was the pastor at the church where Rachel and her mother went. The church has grown quite a bit over the last twenty years, and they have a nice new building about a quarter of a mile south of town."

"Do you think he'd be willing to talk to us?" asked Steve.

"I've served on a few volunteer organizations with him over the years, and he's always seemed pretty reasonable to me. Give him a good reason for asking these questions, and I'm sure he'll answer you."

"Would the reason we gave you do the trick?" Marcie asked.

Mrs. Pritchard smiled. "It's pretty far-fetched, but if the reverend has any curiosity about him, he might be willing to talk as much as he feels he can without violating confidentiality."

"Thanks for meeting with us," Steve said, standing up.

"My pleasure, and I hope I can expect you to stop by when this mystery is solved to let me know what happened."

"I guarantee it," Steve said.

Mrs. Pritchard's face became solemn. "But be careful how you proceed. From what you've told me, there's somebody out there who is willing to use violence to achieve what he or she thinks is a just conclusion to this story."

Chapter Thirteen

Roger Brickmore sat across the table from the police chief, thinking about how many times in the past twenty-five years he had been in this same position, talking over his problems with Grundfeld. He couldn't recall when they first met; sometimes it seemed like Grundfeld had always been there. Not a friend, not a part of the gang: he'd never had anything but contempt for them. In fact, there were times when Brick suspected that Grundfeld even had contempt for him. He'd often wondered how he could separate himself from the man, but there never seemed to be a way that wouldn't cause more harm than good.

They were both nursing cups of coffee in a small diner on the road out of Arbella.

"So the cat got away and was never seen again," Grundfeld concluded with a smile, as if he had finished telling a charming fairy tale.

"And it wasn't Kim's cat?"

"She doesn't have one."

"How did it get into her basement?"

"We took a good long look at her cellar windows. It seems that one of them had been neatly cut out and then put back in place with some putty. So all the person had to do was slip out the piece of glass and toss the cat into the basement. We think that happened after Kim got home, because there was no cat down there when Peters checked the place over."

"But the window had already been cut?"

"Yeah, but it was put back in place so neatly you'd never have noticed it. Whoever it was even put it back in place after they left the cat, and we almost missed it."

"So why the cat?"

Grundfeld shrugged. "Someone knows that Kim Tyler is the nervous sort who will panic at the idea that someone could invade her home in any way. Even though an adult could never have gotten in through that cellar window, finding the strange cat in the house was almost as bad. She started screaming right away that she wanted to be kept under guard in a safe house, like we were U.S. marshals relocating people who testify against the mob."

"What did you do with her?"

"Put her in a motel out by the highway with one officer who stays in the room with her. I can't afford to do that for long, but I'm hoping it won't be necessary for much longer."

Brickmore smiled grimly. "You're figuring that the ghost will come after me next, and you'll catch it."

Grundfeld waved a casual hand. "Stands to reason, don't it?"

"I'm not going to let you do that, Charlie."

"Why not?"

"Think of the headline: BRICKMORE RESCUED FROM VENGEFUL GIRL BY POLICE. I'd be a laughingstock around Hartford."

"Would you rather have BRICKMORE MURDERED: NO CLUES?"

"Plus, having cops around will delay capturing her. Maybe if you hadn't put a guy right outside Kim's house, the ghost would have come knocking and been caught by now."

"So what are you going to do if she shows up?" asked Grundfeld. "Ask her to wait until we arrive?"

Brickmore drew back the side of his jacket and revealed a gun in a holster on his belt.

"What's that, your cell phone?" Grundfeld asked.

"A little something made by Smith & Wesson."

"And about as much use as a cell phone if you don't know how to use it."

"I can use it all right, and I've got a permit to carry it."

Grundfeld smiled in that snide way Brick had come to strongly dislike over the years. He thought it was Grundfeld's way of showing his contempt for him as someone who'd had everything handed to him and didn't know what the struggle of life was all about. *I don't remember seeing that smile when I got him the job as chief of police,* thought Brick. *Then it was all grins and thank-yous.* Where was the gratitude now? Maybe if he thought about it more seriously he'd find a way to free himself of this man.

"Well, don't let that gun make you overconfident. Lots of guys end up getting shot with their own weapons because they underestimate their assailant. Whatever else she may be, this ghost is clever and knows how to surprise people."

Brickmore adjusted his jacket and smiled. "Don't worry. This time I'll be the one doing the surprising."

Grundfeld raised his coffee cup in an ironic salute.

Marcie and Steve parked and looked at the church. Situated in the middle of what had probably once been a farmer's field, the building, more a complex of separate but attached buildings, filled the area. Clearly the chapel was in the center, because the building there had a peaked roof with a cross on top. On either side, lower structures reached out like arms ready to embrace anyone who entered.

The church secretary who had answered the phone told them that the church offices would be to their right as they came in the front door. So they turned right when they entered and went down a short hall to an office marked CHURCH SECRETARY. A pleasant-looking woman looked up and smiled when they came into the office and introduced themselves.

"Pastor Carstairs just came in. Let me buzz him and let him know you're here."

Almost instantly, a man came out of the back office and introduced himself as the pastor. Marcie had expected an older man with a mane of white hair and fierce eyes that would pierce through you to see your soul. But Pastor Carstairs looked to be in early middle age, and his eyes were a mild shade of blue. He escorted them back to his spacious office and closed the door.

Once he was settled behind the desk, he smiled. "According to Ms. Phillips, you're trying to locate a former member of the church."

"Well, actually we are trying to find out what happened

to someone who was a member of this church twenty years ago: Rachel Carpenter."

Marcie thought she saw a frown flash across the minister's face, disturbing the politely helpful expression.

"I remember Rachel. She attended this church for a brief period of time."

"And so did her mother, right?" Marcie asked.

"Correct. They never actually became members. I believe they moved into town in July and attended through December. After that I never saw either one of them again."

"We've been told that Rachel moved away around that time, but her mother remained in town. Did she stop attending this church?"

"Yes," the minister said.

"Do you know why Rachel left town?" Marcie asked pointedly.

The minister leaned back in his chair and looked at them thoughtfully. "Anything else I know about Rachel and her mother I have to consider confidential."

Steve glanced over at Marcie, and she nodded. Steve then told Pastor Carstairs about the ghost haunting Arbella.

"This is all pretty fantastic," the clergyman said when Steve was done. "It's particularly hard to believe that no word of it has leaked out."

"I'm sure you're familiar with Roger Brickmore and the kind of power he has in the town," Steve said.

He nodded. "What I don't understand is where Rachel and her mother fit into all of this."

"From what we've been told, it's possible that Rachel was Brick's girlfriend in the fall of that year. She was also a very close friend of Melissa Harrison's. What we're trying to find out is if there was any connection between Rachel's leaving town and Melissa's death."

"I'm sorry. I really can't tell you any more."

"Was Rachel pregnant and was Roger Brickmore the father?" Marcie asked abruptly, following a sudden inspiration.

The expression of surprise on the clergyman's face gave an affirmative answer.

"I can't tell you that," he said belatedly.

"Let's hypothetically assume that's the case," said Marcie. "Would Rachel have wanted to have the baby? Hypothetically speaking."

Pastor Carstairs paused for a moment, then nodded as if to himself. "Rachel was quite conservative for a young woman, so she would probably want to have the baby."

"Would Roger Brickmore have taken responsibility as the child's father?"

"I think we can assume that."

"Really?" Steve interrupted.

"Speaking hypothetically, love sometimes makes people better than they would otherwise be."

"Then why didn't they get married and live happily ever after?" asked Marcie.

"Think of Romeo and Juliet," Pastor Carstairs said. "It may not be the Good Book, but you can learn a lot from Shakespeare."

"The parents were against it," said Marcie.

"One parent."

"Roger's father?"

The clergyman shook his head.

"But why would Mrs. Carpenter be against it?" asked Steve.

The minister sighed. "Some people complain to me that I preach too much about God's love and not enough about God's justice. Some people feel that the best punishment is the one that takes away from people what they want most."

"Mrs. Carpenter wanted her daughter to suffer for her transgressions, so she refused to let her marry Brick," Marcie said. She thought the minister might have given an almost imperceptible nod of his head.

"Sending her daughter to help take care of her older sister must have seemed a just punishment to her," said Marcie.

"I believe it was very unjust based on Mrs. Carpenter's description of her sister, a woman who apparently made Mrs. Carpenter seem to be the soul of Christian charity," said Carstairs.

"I'll bet Mrs. Carpenter got some money out of Brick's father to take care of the baby," Steve said.

"Speaking speculatively, I believe that Roger's father would have insisted on taking care of the baby financially."

"But why didn't Brick attempt to get in touch with Rachel after the baby was born?" Marcie asked.

"One might hypothesize that Mrs. Carpenter threatened to force Rachel to put the baby up for adoption if Roger ever attempted to contact her."

"What about after the mother died five years ago?" asked Steve.

"That would have been fifteen years after Rachel and Roger had been together. Perhaps by then, Roger's passion had cooled."

"So Rachel gets sent off to be a servant to her aunt, and

Brick is never to have contact with her or the child. Couldn't Rachel have simply refused or come back to town after having the baby?" Steve asked.

The minister shrugged. "Rachel was a very obedient girl. Also, I believe one could be correct in thinking that her mother might have told her that Roger refused to marry her and wanted nothing more to do with her or the baby. Perhaps her aunt was a very intimidating person who kept her under very tight control. At any rate, I never saw Rachel again, nor has anyone in town, to my knowledge."

"Thanks for the information, Pastor Carstairs."

"What information? I really didn't tell you anything. It was all speculation."

"Why were you willing to speculate so freely with us?" Marcie asked.

The minister's lips formed a tight line. "Perhaps because twenty years ago I was unable to sway one of the hardest-hearted people I have ever met."

Chapter Fourteen

Roger Brickmore was smiling to himself as he drove along. Partly it was from the pleasure he took in listening to the sound of his car engine, one of the finest examples of German engineering. He liked it when things went smoothly. He knew that he didn't handle unexpected disruptions well. His father had often told him that he would never be a highly successful businessman because he didn't enjoy the challenge of dealing with the unexpected.

"You're best suited to middle management," his father would say with a sad shake of his head. "You've got a mind that likes the routine and the repetitious. Once emergencies arise, you panic."

Brick had thought that his father's criticism was too harsh then, and he believed that over the years he had become more capable of dealing with sudden change. *Just look at how I've handled this whole ghost thing,* he thought. *I focused on keeping it out of the newspapers, because that was the first priority. Now I've turned my attention to catching whoever is doing this. Once that's been accomplished, the whole matter will be handled quietly and without at lot of negative publicity.*

Once this was over, he'd also find a way of dealing with Grundfeld. Grundfeld's attitude during this Melissa Harrison affair had shown that he was no longer a team player to be relied upon. *His casual, almost mocking, attitude toward my career plans has shown that he no longer sees his future as being tied to my own.* Brick felt himself getting angry, his hands shaking slightly on the leather steering wheel. But he calmed himself by rehashing the idea he'd had the previous night on how to deal with Grundfeld. He'd heard all the rumors about how the chief was involved in most of the illegal activities that took place in town. If he secretly went to the governor and expressed his concern about what Grundfeld was doing, he knew that the state police would conduct an undercover investigation. Hopefully that would put Grundfeld in jail without making public Brickmore's own involvement. The last thing he wanted was Grundfeld coming out of jail with a grudge against him.

He stepped harder on the gas as he took the road that forked up the hill to the high school. An emergency meeting of the school board had been called because of the need to reduce the budget further. As the only local political position he'd held, Brick took it seriously as proof to those in Hartford that he had paid his dues at the grassroots level. He was about halfway up the hill when he saw the car pulled off to the side of the road. She had already jacked up the left rear and was getting ready to remove the lug nuts from the wheel, a job that could prove dirty and make him late for the meeting. Brickmore nonetheless pulled off to the side in front of her car. She was attractive and might even prove helpful in the future.

As he walked back toward her, she glanced up from where she was wrestling with the tire iron and gave him an embarrassed smile.

"Need some help?" he asked, trying to sound avuncular rather than condescending.

"Thanks. I think I've got these, but I should have taken the spare out of the trunk before I jacked the car up. It's one of those donuts, so it isn't very heavy."

"I think I can handle it," Brickmore said with a grin.

He walked to the trunk and began to peel back the floor covering to get at the spare when he was suddenly aware the she was standing right next to him. *This may prove more worthwhile than I thought,* he said to himself, imagining that asking her out on a date after helping her change a tire would be a natural transition.

She slipped the long, narrow blade between his ribs and shoved hard until she was certain that it had pierced his heart. He made a low, soft sound like a polite cough and fell toward her. She let him lean against her and pulled out the blade, carefully placing it on a piece of plastic in the trunk. She put his left arm over her shoulder and her right arm around his waist and dragged him to the edge of the road, thankful that on Saturdays this road was almost unused. When she reached the shoulder of the road, she shoved him off the embankment and watched the body roll down into the underbrush. Her call to his house the night before, announcing the phony surprise meeting, had worked well.

Never having really loosened the lug nuts at all, it only took her five minutes to stow away the jack and be on her way. As she drove down the hill, she experienced a moment's satisfaction that the job was finally done, then smiled in anticipation of the commotion that Brickmore's death would cause in Arbella.

Chapter Fifteen

Tracy Harrison, Melissa's mother, sat on the sofa across from Steve and Marcie and looked at them expectantly. She had agreed to see them when they called and said they were working on a story about Melissa's death. But her first question to them was why they were interested in doing a story now, so she obviously had no knowledge of the ghost attacks. Marcie and Steve had agreed in advance that if she didn't already know, they wouldn't tell her. First of all, she probably wouldn't believe it, and second, it would upset her.

Steve cleared his throat. "Well, Mrs. Harrison, I guess the main reason is that it's the twenty-year anniversary of the crime and it still hasn't been solved. We thought it was only fitting to write an article reminding people of the crime and talking about where the investigation stands right now."

"I can tell you where it stands right now. The same place it stood twenty years ago when the police were too cowardly to charge Roger Brickmore with the murder of my daughter."

"You're convinced that he was the murderer?" asked Marcie.

The woman nodded. "I was always suspicious of why he wanted to go out with Melissa. We aren't wealthy, and we didn't travel in the same social circle as the Brickmores. I thought he should have stayed with his own kind."

"But he had a lot of friends at school who weren't wealthy," Steve pointed out.

"You mean that little group that used to always be around him. The same ones who gave him an alibi for my Melissa's death. They were just some kids that he lorded over. They hung around him for what they could get. Melissa was never like that. That's why I told her to stay away from Brick."

"How did Brick treat Melissa?" asked Marcie.

"Oh, all right, I guess," she said with a shrug. "At least, Melissa never told me about anything he did that was wrong. But I knew it would happen eventually. At that age, you know what every boy wants from a pretty girl, and in Roger's case, he probably thought he deserved it because he was better than everyone else. There had always been rumors about him around the high school. Melissa knew about them; that's why she put him off the first few times he asked her out. The first time she actually went out with him, they double-dated with a couple of Melissa's friends. When he behaved himself, she started to date him regularly."

"Melissa was a very pretty girl. Didn't she already have a boyfriend?" asked Marcie.

The woman nodded. "She'd been going out with Mike Tolliver for most of her junior year. But then Mike got into an auto accident in the fall and was charged with driving under the influence, so we told Melissa that she couldn't go out with him anymore." She looked across the room through tear-filled eyes. "You don't know how many times her father and I wished that we'd never done that. But it seemed like the responsible thing to do at the time."

"Do you think she was serious about Brick?" Marcie asked.

"She liked him well enough, but I don't think she was in love with him. I think she still loved Mike and was hoping that if he got his act together, we'd eventually change our minds about him. The other thing was that Brick had been Rachel's boyfriend."

"Rachel Carpenter?" asked Steve.

"Right. She and Melissa were pretty good friends during the first half of their senior year. Rachel had just moved into the area, and Melissa was the kind of girl who would always try to make people feel welcome." Mrs. Harrison paused and poked at her eyes with a tissue. "She didn't want Rachel to be lonely, so she made friends with her. That couldn't have been easy, because Rachel was a very quiet girl."

"Did they have things in common?" asked Marcie.

"They were both good students, and both of them liked to read. Rachel was a nice girl, but she had a hard time at home. We had her over to supper one evening when her mother had to work late. I got a call from her mother the next day asking that we not invite Rachel to our house because she didn't want her daughter exposed to an environment that didn't have the same values as her own. I can tell you, it was all I could do to keep from tearing off a piece of that woman. No wonder poor Rachel was so quiet. She told Melissa that she was surprised we talked at mealtime, because her mother never spoke. I'm sure she thought she was a very religious woman, but I think she was just sick."

"And Rachel went out with Brick during the fall. How did that ever happen?" asked Steve.

"Melissa never understood it either. All of a sudden, Brick started talking to Rachel before and after class. He would walk next to her in the hall. She tried to ignore him at first, even told him to go away. But Brick was persistent, and, to be honest, he could be a charming boy. He was smart and funny when he wanted to be."

"But could they actually have dated? Mrs. Carpenter wouldn't have allowed it, would she?" said Marcie.

"I doubt it. She worked at the mill owned by Brick's father, but I don't think that would have stopped her from telling Brick to get lost. I suspect they must have spent time together right after school before her mother got home from work. Brick had a car, so they could have gone anywhere."

"And then suddenly, after Christmas, Rachel was gone," Marcie said.

"I was surprised how much that shocked Melissa. I hadn't realized what good friends they'd become. Melissa called Rachel's mother and asked where she was. All the woman would tell her was that Rachel was taking care of an elderly aunt in Maine. When Melissa asked for an address to write to, the woman said that she wanted Rachel to make a clean break from her old school."

"Did Melissa ever say anything more about why Rachel left?"

"Not to me. I think she asked Brick about it, and he said he had no idea except that her mother was a witch. Actually, one of the odd things about Melissa's relationship with Brick is that they spent a lot of time talking about Rachel.

There were times when I wondered if they cared about each other or just wanted to keep some connection to her."

"Do you have any idea what Melissa and Roger were arguing about at the prom?" asked Marcie.

Mrs. Harrison shook her head. "They never seemed to argue, so I had no idea what it could have been about. All I know is that Melissa seemed very odd on the day of the prom."

"Odd in what way?" asked Steve.

"Preoccupied, as if she had something on her mind. And when Brick came to pick her up, she was rather short with him. I think he was surprised. The only thing was that just before she came downstairs to see Brick, I saw her stuffing a letter in the small bag she was taking to the prom."

"And you have no idea why someone would have wanted to hurt her?" asked Marcie.

"As I told you, I always thought it had to be Roger. She must have said something that set him off. I always thought his polite outside manner hid an inner violence." She paused and swallowed hard. "If only we'd been home when Melissa called, we wouldn't be wondering about all this. And Melissa would still be alive."

"Some people talked about a passing stranger who might have attacked her."

"If any stranger had tried to pick her up, Melissa would have run away. She was on track and field. Nobody would have caught her, even without shoes and in a prom dress. Whoever killed her was someone she knew." She sighed. "I don't really want to talk about this anymore. Not after all the years Melissa's father and I went over and over what happened. Then he'd sit it that chair," she said, indicating a tired recliner in the corner of the room, "and I knew he was just going over and over in his mind why he hadn't been home when his daughter called. When the terminal cancer diagnosis came, I think he was almost relieved."

Marcie and Steve said good-bye. They walked back to the car and sat there without speaking.

Finally Marcie said, "You know, that's a real tragedy. There's just no way you can find any good coming out of it. They didn't do anything wrong, but because of what they did, their daughter is dead. I'm not sure how you do go on living with something like that."

"Do you think she's right about Brick killing Melissa?" asked Steve.

"I'm figuring Melissa got a letter from Rachel telling her about the pregnancy and maybe telling her how miserable she was living with her aunt."

"No wonder Brick said he had been unfaithful to Melissa with Cindy Gower, and that's what they were fighting over. As bad as that sounds, it's better than abandoning your pregnant girlfriend," said Steve. "But wait a minute, why would Melissa get angry at Brick? After all, he'd wanted to marry Rachel. It was her mother who prevented it."

"But according to Reverend Carstairs, Rachel never knew that."

"Why not?"

"Like he said, only Mr. Brickmore, Mrs. Carpenter, and he himself knew what the final agreement was. So maybe Rachel's mother told her that Brick wouldn't agree to marry her and that she was sending her out of state to have the baby."

"Why would she say that?"

"Because it was the only way she could think of to punish her daughter and avoid the embarrassment of having the town know that—as she would think of it—she had failed as a mother. That's why she didn't let Brick and Rachel marry. In her mind, that would be rewarding sin. And the best way to punish Rachel was to have her think that the boy who got her pregnant wanted nothing more to do with her."

"That's pretty cold."

"And the results were terrible, because by doing that she set events in motion that would lead to Melissa's death."

"How?"

"Because when Rachel wrote to Melissa, she would have painted a very negative picture of Brick. That led directly to Melissa's confrontation with Brick at the dance and her death."

Steve's cell phone rang. He answered and Marcie saw his face go blank.

"Okay, okay, we'll be there," Steve said.

"What was that about?" Marcie asked.

"Roger Brickmore is dead. He's been murdered."

"By the ghost?"

Steve shrugged. "Don't know. That was a friend of mine at the *Arbella Beacon*. He says that he just got a briefing by Chief Grundfeld. He owes me a favor, so if we meet him for a cup of coffee in twenty minutes, he'll tell me all he knows."

"Well, I guess that will give us the proper end to our story."

"No," said Steve, "the proper end will be when we find who's been playing ghost and why."

Chapter Sixteen

Charlie Grundfeld sat behind his desk and smiled. It was unusual to have things work out so much better than he could have expected, and he wanted to savor the moment. He had never anticipated that Brick would actually be murdered. Whatever negative publicity this resulted in for the police department could easily be deflected by saying that the victim had refused police protection. And, more important, it opened up a whole new world of opportunities for him.

Grundfeld thought about the future. He didn't do this sort of thing frequently. His plans were usually created while on the run and were short-term, covering the next week or month. But Brick's death had extended his horizon. Although Brick had been helpful while Grundfeld was making his way up the ladder in the police department, Roger had made it quite clear to the chief of police that that was where his ambitions would have to stop. Brick wanted him in that job to prevent even the remote possibility of the Harrison case being reopened.

Now, with Brick gone, Grundfeld was free to imagine a life beyond police work. One idea that had occasionally fluttered through his mind—it would be saying too much to claim that he had truly thought about it—was the possibility of becoming mayor. He knew that he was pretty popular with the more conservative elements in town, and he spoke well in public. All in all, he looked and sounded like the kind of guy who would get things done.

Mayoral terms were only two years, and he knew that department regulations would allow him to take unpaid leave to serve as mayor. If he liked it, and if it looked like it might lead to higher political office, he'd run for re-election. If not, he could always go back to being chief. The only drawback was that by stepping down as chief, he would have to give up all the lucrative illegal activities that resulted from his present position. He pondered the problem. He could recommend Steinholtz as acting chief. He had lots of seniority and was popular with the men. Fortunately, he was also slow witted, so it would be unlikely that he would crack down on corruption. But Grundfeld knew he would still need someone in the department to be his eyes and ears.

He liked the way Jena Conway was working out. Although his view of women generally was that they were only good for one thing, he'd actually found himself enjoying her company as his driver. She was easy on the eyes, but more important, he detected a certain tough shrewdness in her that he thought might make them good partners in crime. He'd have to think of a subtle way to approach her that would not put him in obvious jeopardy but would still make clear what he was offering her. Who knew, he thought with a smile, in a few years she might become chief, making the department look more tolerant than it was in reality and allowing him to keep making money.

There was a knock on the door, and Jena Conway walked in. For one wild moment, he considered hinting at what the future might offer both of them, but prudence limited him to asking her what she wanted.

"I have a report on what we've got so far from the scene of the crime. Apparently there was another car parked there, but the driver was very careful to obliterate any tire tracks. We went up to the high school to see if anyone had driven up the road during the late afternoon, but no luck there. There was one janitor who had been there since the morning, and no athletic practices were scheduled."

"What was Brick doing heading up there in the first place?" asked Grundfeld.

Jena shrugged. "No idea. Maybe someone called and arranged to meet him there."

"You mean this ghost called him and set up a date? She didn't do that with anyone else."

"She didn't kill anyone else, either," Jena pointed out.

"That's because she thought that Brickmore was the one actually responsible for Melissa Harrison's death." Grundfeld sighed and shook his head. "All because of a baby. What bothers me is why Brick would stop for her in the first place, and even more, why would he let her get the drop on him? He had a gun, for crying out loud. How did she ever get close enough to shove a blade in him?"

"We'll know that when we catch her."

The chief sighed. "If we ever do. She's done what she wanted to do: gotten her revenge. Now she'll probably just disappear, and we'll have Brick's death as an open case along with Harrison's. Only this will be worse, because

Brick is a somebody, and the state boys will be here and never let it rest as long as they can milk it for some publicity."

Jena smiled. "Don't worry, Chief. Roger Brickmore didn't have a wife or family. They're the ones who never forget and keep these things alive. I'd bet that in less than a month this is ancient history."

Grundfeld gave her a look of admiration. "I never thought of that. I bet you're right."

Steve and Marcie slid into the booth across from Steve's friend. Steve introduced him as Mike Price. The man, who appeared to be in his early thirties, was thin to the point of emaciation, even managing to make Steve look a trifle overweight. He reached a hand across to Marcie. She noticed his nicotine-stained fingers and kept contact to a minimum.

"Okay, here's what I've got, and this is what we're going to run tomorrow morning. Person or persons unknown stabbed Roger Brickmore to death on the road up to the high school on Saturday afternoon. Police are currently investigating. The rest of the article will be filler about what Roger Brickmore's done in his life, leaving out most of the bad stuff that we can't prove."

"What about the earlier attacks by the ghost?" asked Marcie.

"Yeah, we've got all that information too. We couldn't run it when Roger Brickmore was alive, or he, along with Grundfeld, would have crushed us. Now that Brick is dead and there's no close family to protect his good name, we're thinking about running with it. But we'll wait a day or two to make sure there won't be any blowback."

"What is Grundfeld's view on that?" asked Steve.

"At the press conference, I kind of asked him if we could put the death in the context of other recent attacks. He said that as long as we stuck with the facts, he'd have no complaints.

"I have to run now," Mike said. He looked at the check on the table as if it were a dead roach.

"Don't worry, I'll take care of it," said Steve.

"You're a pal," Mike said, and then, with a nod to Marcie, he slipped out of the booth.

"What did he have to eat?" Marcie asked.

Steve studied the check. "Looks like a cheeseburger and fries."

"I think you got robbed."

"Maybe not. I'm thinking that if Grundfeld doesn't care what comes out now, we can talk to Brick's pals. They might be willing to say more now. It will help us beef up the story."

"I think we already know all there is to find out about the ghost attacks," said Marcie.

"I was thinking more about what happened at that prom twenty years ago."

"You figure someone might know more than they were saying."

"Well, I think that when Brick was alive, they had a good reason to edit their comments. It would be interesting to find out if anything has changed."

Steve took out his cell phone, scrolled down the listings, and punched in the number.

"Hello, Mr. Morgan, this is Steve Rostow from the *Arbella Archives*. I wanted to offer my condolences on the death of Roger Brickmore. I'm working on his obituary, and I was wondering if I could meet with you to get some of your personal reminiscences."

Steve paused. Then he said, "That will be fine. I'll see you then."

"You're going to talk with Buster," said Marcie.

"Yeah. I figure he's the dumbest of the group, so he might tell me more than the others. Plus, he might have gotten the sharp side of Brick's tongue more often because he worked for him. So he might be interested in getting some of his own back. Tomorrow we'll talk to the others."

Marcie shook her head. "I have to leave tomorrow morning. I'm supposed to be back at work by Monday."

"Aw, come on, Marcie. Call your boss and tell her that you need another day because this thing is heating up."

"I don't know. I've already gotten more time from Amanda than she probably wanted to give me."

"You'll never know unless you try."

"Okay," Marcie agreed reluctantly.

She grabbed her cell phone and walked outside the coffee shop. She put in Amanda's home number, but there was no answer. She tried the office, and Amanda answered. Once the greetings were out of the way, Marcie got straight to the point.

"I'd like to stay up here one more day. A murder has just been committed, probably by the person pretending to be the ghost."

"Will one more day make much of a difference? The investigation could go on for weeks," Amanda said.

"You're right. But tomorrow Steve and I can interview some of the dead man's friends. I think that will pretty much complete the research for the story. Steve can write it up, and if anything new happens before the story goes to the printer, we'll work it in somehow."

"Okay. But I'm really falling behind on the editing for the next issue. Have you finished the ones I assigned to you?"

"I brought them with me on the laptop. They're all done."

She heard Amanda breathe a sigh of relief. "Great. Well, then, I guess you can stay through Sunday and drive back on Monday, but be here bright and early Tuesday morning. Sorry to be hassling you so much, but being shorthanded is no fun."

"I know. And I wouldn't ask to stay down here if things weren't starting to break."

"Okay. Well, I hope you and Steve get a good story. And be careful."

"Will do."

Marcie went back into the coffee shop and slid into the booth across from Steve.

"So, what's the story?" he asked.

Marcie smiled. "Let's go bust Buster."

Chapter Seventeen

It turned out that Buster Morgan lived in the only high-rise building in Arbella. You knew it was a high-rise because a sign prominently displayed by the front door said HIGH-RISE CONDOMINIUMS FOR SALE. Otherwise, you might have had doubts, because the building only soared twelve stories into the air. Marcie wasn't sure if there was some minimum number of stories you had to have to call yourself a high-rise, but she had a feeling that this building wouldn't make it.

The lobby was done in a combination of tile and faux marble. One wall was given over to a bank of mailboxes. Opposite that was the elevator. Steve pushed the button and smiled at Marcie.

"I think you should lead the way here."

"Why?"

"Well, aside from having a well-deserved reputation as a drinker, Buster also has a reputation as something of a ladies' man. I'm not sure how well deserved that one is, but I know he likes to talk to women. Just flatter him a little, and he'll tell us all we want to know."

Buster's apartment was on the twelfth floor, directly across from the elevator.

"Having his door near the elevator has probably saved Buster lots of nights when he's staggered home blind drunk," said Steve.

Marcie rang the bell. After a long minute, the door opened, and Buster stood there with a drink in his hand. He was tall and broad-shouldered, but what you noticed first was the sizable belly hanging over his belt buckle. He had a full head of dark hair liberally mixed with gray, and his face had the florid look of the active drinker, as Marcie knew from seeing some of her father's friends in the military.

"Come in, come in," he said, giving Marcie an overly elaborate bow while at the same time ignoring Steve. "Can I get you a drink?" he asked as soon as they reached the center of the living room. He had a hand on Marcie's elbow.

"No, thank you," Marcie said, walking quickly away from him to look out the window. "You have a wonderful view from here," she said, although what you actually saw the most of was the interstate highway that ran right past the building.

"Yes, indeed. Of course, I rarely have time to enjoy it because of my job, and then I do have a rather active social life that keeps me out most evenings and much of the weekend. But please sit down."

Marcie and Steve sat on either end of a cream-colored sofa. The whole room was done in whites and off-whites.

Marcie wondered whether he'd had a decorator or had inherited this from the previous owner.

"You work at Brickmore Industries, don't you?" she asked.

Buster nodded and took a sip of his drink. "I'm associate manager of public relations. How an enterprise is perceived by the public is very important today," he recited, as if he'd memorized the lines from a training manual.

Marcie smiled. "I guess Roger Brickmore trusted you with such an important position because you were an old friend."

"Well, of course, friend or not, I had to earn that trust," Buster said earnestly. "I've worked at Brickmore's for almost sixteen years, and I like to think that I've proven myself over and over again."

"But I'm sure your friendship with Roger didn't hurt?"

Buster gave a self-satisfied chuckle. "*Who* you know gives you a chance to prove *what* you know, as I always say. And you're right. Roger and I were very tight in high school. There was a small group of us that went almost everywhere with Brick."

"You had a chance to enjoy the good life?" Marcie asked.

"You bet. He'd take us out on his boat on the lake. We'd stay at his chalet in the winter and go skiing. Wherever we went, it was nothing but the best. He was a great buddy."

It suddenly seemed to occur to Buster that he should show more sorrow for the loss of his friend. He put his drink down on the end table, and a hand went up to his brow. "You can understand why this is a particularly difficult time for me."

Marcie nodded and tried to smile sympathetically.

"I imagine that you must consider yourself to be rather lucky," Marcie said.

The hand went down to reveal a puzzled expression.

"Lucky? Why do you say that?"

"Not just you, of course, but all the other members of that little group of friends who were close to Roger in high school. All of you were attacked by Melissa's ghost, but only Roger was killed."

"Sure, but there's no reason why the ghost would want to kill us."

"But there was a reason why the ghost would want to kill Roger. Like maybe Roger murdered Melissa, and you guys all covered up for him."

Buster took a long swig from his drink. His hand shook slightly as he set it back on the table.

"I didn't mean it that way. As far as I know, Brick had nothing to do with the death of the Harrison girl. What I was trying to say is that the ghost might think he was the one."

"You believe Melissa's ghost wouldn't know who killed her?" Marcie asked. "Not a very smart ghost."

Buster laughed and shook a finger at her. "I don't believe in ghosts and I don't think you do either, little lady," he said in a singsong voice. "Somebody is pretending to be her ghost, and I'm saying that person has it wrong."

"Still, it must have been pretty scary seeing the ghost in the parking lot that night."

A somber expression came over Buster and he shook himself. "You can't imagine what a shock it was to see this girl in that pretty dress with blood all over the front of her. I kept seeing it over and over again at night for weeks

afterward." He held up his glass. "Even a stiff nightcap didn't help."
"Did she look a lot like Melissa?" Marcie asked.
"I don't know. I hardly looked at her face once I saw all that blood and the knife in her hand."
Marcie paused as a question came to her. "Did you think it was Melissa when you first saw her?"
Buster sipped his drink and stared across the off-white carpet like it was the Siberian tundra.
"I didn't really know Melissa all that well. Brick had only been going out with her for a few months before the prom, and she didn't mix with us. We were Brick's friends; she was just a girlfriend. They came and went."
"Like Rachel?"
"Yeah, I never got to know her, either."
"So what did you think when you saw the ghost if you didn't think it was Melissa?"
"I'm not sure what I thought. There was this woman covered in blood coming at me with a knife. All I thought was 'Let's get the heck out of here.' "
"Did you tell the paramedics that Melissa's ghost attacked you?"
"I was in shock. I really don't know what I said to them."
"Can you recall when you first started to think that it was Melissa's ghost?"
"I know that I said something to Chief Grundfeld about it being her ghost, and he made fun of me for believing in ghosts. But that would have been later, when I was in my hospital room. I bet Grundfeld isn't laughing so much now that Brick is dead."
"Why not?"

"He was a friend of Brick's too. That's how he got his job."

"Let's go back to the prom for a moment," said Steve. "You, Penny, and Kim said that you saw Roger at the dance between eight thirty and ten o'clock. Am I right?"

"Sure. I mean, none of us was with him the whole time. But one or the other of us was either with him or saw him around during that time."

"Roger and Melissa argued just before eight thirty, and then she left."

"Yeah. She was all upset about something the whole night. Then I saw her and Roger in the corner, and I could tell they were fighting. She walked out of the gym, and I don't know where she went."

"Roger didn't follow her?"

"Nope."

"Could he have left the dance for five minutes between eight thirty and ten o'clock without any of you noticing?"

"Yeah, I suppose so."

"Ten minutes?"

"Maybe."

"What about fifteen?"

"Look, I don't know what you're getting at, but it would have taken a lot more than fifteen minutes to catch Melissa, kill her, and get back to the prom. One of us would have noticed."

"Yeah. But would you have told the police?" asked Steve.

Buster waved a disgusted hand in his direction. "Hey, I don't like what you're implying."

"What did Roger and Melissa fight about?" asked Marcie.

"I thought you guys were going to write a tribute to

Roger. This is sounding more and more like a criminal investigation. I don't want to say any more."

"Afraid of getting yourself in trouble?"

"No. I didn't do anything wrong."

Buster lurched to his feet, marched across the living room, and opened the door. He moved his head to show that they should leave.

"I'm sure you're going to miss Roger," Steve said as he walked out into the hall.

"Of course I am. He was my friend," Buster said.

"You have an even better reason than that."

"What?"

"Somebody else is going to be running Brickmore Industries now, and he or she might not think they need an associate manager of public relations."

A worried look came over Buster's face as he closed the door.

"There was something he said that didn't fit," Marcie said, as they rode down on the elevator.

"Didn't fit with what?"

"That's the thing, I'm not sure."

"The only thing I'm pretty sure of is that Buster probably doesn't know much more than he's saying."

"Maybe one of the other ones will."

"Let's hope."

Chapter Eighteen

It was late afternoon when Marcie returned to the motel. Since she now planned to stay another night, she went in the office to see if her room would be available for Sunday night. Lisa came out of the back room at the sound of the bell over the door.

"What can I do for you?" she asked in a voice that hoped the answer would be "nothing at all."

I'm happy to see you again too, Marcie thought.

"I've decided to stay through Sunday. Can I have the same room for tomorrow night?"

Lisa looked through numerous pieces of paper on the counter as if that might not be possible.

"You don't have to register again, because I've still got your card, but I'm going to have to move you today."

"Why?"

"Your room is scheduled for its monthly cleaning."

Marcie decided she didn't want to know.

"Are you going to be leaving early in the morning on Monday?"

"Why?"

"I'm putting you on the far end from the office, so you can pull right out without waking other people. Don't bother turning in the key. Just leave it in the room on the dresser."

"I don't know how early I'm going to be leaving. But I'll do it that way if you want."

"Yeah, it's easier for me. You might want to think about getting out of here before nine. The guy who takes care of the grounds will be around by then, and he makes a lot of noise. You can hardly hear yourself think."

"Thanks for the advice."

Marcie went back to her old room and packed her things, then pulled her car down to the space in front of her new room and hauled her luggage out of the trunk. *Every time I see Lisa,* Marcie thought, *she's trying to get me to move along. I wonder what she's trying to hide.* Once again, Marcie wondered whether Lisa was the one playing Melissa's ghost. Marcie'd have to find out more about Lisa to discover the answer to that.

After getting set up in her new room, Marcie sat in the single straight-backed chair provided and thought about what they'd discovered today. She actually agreed with Buster that the death of Roger was no surprise. It was sort of the culmination of the attacks on all the others. The ghost clearly thought that Roger was guilty of Melissa's death. But who would bother to take that kind of revenge twenty years later? There was also something in what Buster had told her about recognizing the ghost as being Melissa's that bothered her. Marcie couldn't put her finger on it, but somehow it had raised a flag.

As Marcie thought about what had been discovered so

far, it came together like this: Brick had gotten Rachel pregnant, but he hadn't married her, because her mother wouldn't agree to it. Rachel had gone off to Maine to take care of her aunt. This much Marcie was certain of, but the rest relied more on speculation. Somehow, probably by mail, Rachel had contacted Melissa shortly before the prom and told her about the pregnancy. Melissa had gotten furious, and at the dance, she'd accused Roger of being a cad. She had stormed out of the prom and started to walk home. Along the way, someone had murdered her.

That mysterious someone was still the problem. Melissa had probably threatened to tell everyone about the pregnancy to embarrass Roger if he wouldn't marry her friend. Roger hadn't wanted all of this to come out in the open, so he'd murdered her. That still seemed like the best explanation. Even though people had seen him at the prom between the time when Melissa left and when her body was found, there was really no guarantee that he hadn't slipped away sometime. It would, however, have been hard for him to be gone long enough to commit the murder without its being noticed, if his friends were telling the truth. Melissa had probably tried to call home from a pay phone at the school, and when she hadn't gotten an answer, she'd started walking. Someone had followed her and killed her less than a hundred yards from the school. So, Marcie thought, the odds were that she'd died closer to nine o'clock than to ten. But that didn't clear things up very much.

But if it wasn't Brick, who could it be? Maybe one of his friends. She doubted it was one of the women, although she immediately thought that might be a sexist assumption. She didn't see Buster cutting anyone's throat. He hardly seemed capable of cutting his meat. She'd never met James.

But since he was a veterinarian, he might be more competent with a knife. It might be worthwhile talking to him.

But even if she could come up with evidence as to who had killed Melissa, that wouldn't tell her who had just murdered Brickmore. Obviously, it had been someone who wanted revenge and thought Brick was a killer. Someone who was clever enough and had a streak of cruelty that made him—or her—want to toy with the victim by attacking the others first. Aside for some vague suspicions regarding Lisa, Marcie had no idea who that could be.

Marcie and Steve had agreed to get together for breakfast in the morning to finalize the details on the story he was going to write. She hoped Steve would find the writing rewarding and not be too disappointed by the low pay and the fact that it wouldn't make him a household name. She was still unsure how much to encourage Steve in his writing career. He had the benefit of a secure job, something she wouldn't mind having right now herself. And even if Steve didn't find teaching high school to be very exciting, he could always supplement both his income and his creative desires by writing the occasional article for a magazine. Plus, there was always the *Arbella Archives.*

Marcie's cell phone rang. It was Steve.

"Hi, Marcie. I was over here at the *Arbella Archives* working on something when Jena Conway stopped by. She's off duty tonight and wanted to know if we'd be interested in having dinner with her at her apartment."

"Sounds a lot better than eating alone in some fast-food place," Marcie said.

"Okay. I'll pick you up around six."

After she hung up, Marcie started her computer and turned to an article that would be coming out two issues down the road. The more she could get done ahead of time, the less Amanda and she would have to worry about closer to the date of publication. She knew that Amanda would only let her engage in these prolonged investigations if she kept up-to-date with her proofreading, so multitasking on the road was essential. This was more important than ever now that their staff had been cut.

At five thirty Marcie put on her last set of clean clothes, a light blue scoop-necked tank top and a pair of jeans; then over the tank top, she put on a darker blue long-sleeved T-shirt. She was waiting in the doorway of her room when Steve appeared five minutes later.

"That's one of the things I like about you," Steve said as she got in the car.

"What's that?"

"You never keep a guy waiting."

"That's the best you can do for a compliment? Nothing about my wit or beauty?"

"I didn't want to embarrass you with too much praise."

"I can take it," she said, and they both laughed.

"I didn't realize you were such a good friend of Jena's that she would invite you over for dinner."

"She's mentioned it a few times. Actually, I think that the fact that you're in town makes it easier for her, because she can invite me over without having it seem like a date."

"You don't think she's interested?"

"Just in being a friend. The story of my life."

Steve laughed, but Marcie felt that this was a comment on their relationship as well.

They made a right turn just outside of town and went down a road that led into a condominium community. Jena's address was the tenth door on the right.

"Hi. Did you find me without any trouble?" Jena asked as she opened the door and ushered them inside.

"As long as we had the number there was no problem," said Steve. "Otherwise, they all look alike."

Jena nodded. "I know. I'm not much of a drinker, but I think it would be a real challenge for someone who was drunk and couldn't remember the number. You'd probably have to get out of the car and count the doors."

When they got inside, Jena took them on a quick tour of the place. Marcie thought the rooms were large, but all looked like they could use a coat of paint, and Jena didn't seem to have much furniture. Other than a sofa and one chair in the living room and a card table with four folding chairs that served as the dining table, there was nothing on the first floor. On the second floor, she had a bed in the largest bedroom and one chest of drawers. The other rooms were empty.

"So what do you think?" Jena asked.

"Very spacious," Marcie said.

"This is the kind of place that I need," Steve added.

"I know I don't have much furniture, and the whole place can use work. But I only got the condo six months ago, and I've been so busy that there's been no time to even do the basics."

"Were you renting before that?" asked Marcie.

Jena nodded. "But you pay so much rent and get nothing to show for it that I decided to invest in a place of my own." She turned to Steve. "You could buy something like this. With your teacher's salary, there'd be no problem."

"It has one big advantage over where I am right now," he said.

"What?" Jena asked.

"Privacy," Steve said in a prayerlike voice. "What I wouldn't do for privacy."

When everyone was seated in the living room, Jena said, "I'm not much of a cook, but there are a couple of things I do well, and one of them is spaghetti and meatballs. So if you'll excuse me for a moment while I put the spaghetti on, we'll be eating in about fifteen minutes."

"So you think you'd like a place like this?" Marcie asked Steve.

"Sure."

"Then why don't you have one?"

"Like I told you before, that would be committing myself to staying here and teaching. I'd be giving up on my life as a writer."

"Couldn't you keep doing what you're doing on the *Arbella Archives* even if you had a condo?"

"Sure."

"Couldn't you keep looking for a job as a writer?"

"I suppose so."

"And if you did get a job and had to move, couldn't you sell the condo?"

"I guess, but what's your point?"

"My point is that you don't have to live in your parents' basement in order to become a writer. You seem to think that if you make any commitment to living here in Arbella, you'll have to give up your goal to write. I'm just saying you can pursue both at the same time. You can settle down here but keep looking for other opportunities."

Steve shook his head. "I'm afraid that slowly but surely I'll become content, and twenty years from now I'll be a high school teacher who has never done much else."

"It doesn't have to be that way if you don't let it. Plus,

I'm not sure how bad a job it is teaching high school. If you do it well, it certainly seems as rewarding as being an editor. And to be absolutely honest, I wouldn't mind having some of your financial security."

Steve didn't say anything. At first Marcie was afraid that she had offended him, but when she looked over, he seemed to be lost in thought.

Marcie didn't consider herself an expert on Italian food. Her mother had cooked in a certain Midwestern style in which everything was white, due to cheese or cream sauce or both. But Jena's spaghetti and meatballs seemed very authentic to her. The conversation over dinner covered a number of things. Steve told several good stories about his students and happenings in the high school, Jena had a couple of tales about the police department, and Marcie talked about several of her more recent investigations. Eventually, however, the conversation came back to the story they were writing about Melissa's murder.

"I think something is about to break," Steve said with a gleam in his eye.

"I don't know how you can think that. Now that Brick is dead, the ghost will probably disappear back into the woodwork. The police don't have any clues, do they?" Marcie asked Jena.

Jena gave a small smile. "I shouldn't really say anything, but no, we don't. All we know is that there was a car parked there, and Brickmore stopped for some reason and was murdered."

"If it was the ghost, he wouldn't have stopped. Or he'd at least have been very careful to defend himself," said Marcie.

"He was carrying a gun, and it wasn't even drawn from its holster," Jena pointed out.

"So he was taken completely by surprise," Marcie said.

"Maybe by someone he knew," Steve added.

Jena shrugged and gave them a good-humored smile. "All this speculation is fine, and you both may be right. But the police need evidence. Right now that's sorely lacking."

"I think we'll learn a lot more if we follow up on the Rachel pregnancy lead," Steve said.

Jena stopped spinning the spaghetti onto her fork. "What's this all about?" she asked.

Steve blushed. "Marcie and I have been following up on a couple of leads on our own. I haven't seen you recently to tell you about them."

"Well, maybe you'd better tell me now," Jena said with a sudden firmness in her voice.

Steve and Marcie took turns telling what they had learned from Pastor Carstairs and Mrs. Harrison.

"Roger wanted to marry Rachel, but her mother wouldn't hear of it," Jena said.

"According to the reverend."

Jena coughed and cleared her throat. "So Roger's former girlfriend was pregnant and got sent away by her mother to have the baby and never returned. But you think that somehow Melissa heard about the pregnancy right before the prom."

"Remember that Melissa was this girl's best friend," Steve said.

"Okay. So Melissa confronts Roger during the dance, and that's what the argument everyone reported was about," said Jena.

"Right," Steve said, cutting off another piece of the crusty Italian bread. "I'm sure Melissa would have been furious at the way her friend was treated, and she was probably angry at Roger for not telling her that he had gotten Rachel pregnant."

"And Melissa is so angry that when she can't reach anyone at home for a ride, she decides to walk home from the dance," said Jena.

"She was an athlete in track and field, so it would have probably seemed very doable to her," Marcie added.

Jena sat back and studied the two of them. "So, what happened next?"

Steve and Marcie looked at each other. After a moment Steve spoke. "We don't know for sure. Maybe Brick chased after Melissa and killed her. The trouble with that theory is that Brick's friends say they saw him frequently in the time between when Melissa left the dance and the finding of her body."

"Do you believe them?" Jena asked.

Steve shrugged. "I guess I think they may have exaggerated the number of times they saw him, and he could have committed the murder."

"But he must have been very fast," added Marcie. "Maybe he left right after Melissa did and got ahead of her when she stopped to call home, and then he waited for her along the road and killed her. If the whole thing took no more than ten minutes, I guess Brick could have done it."

"But we aren't sure that's what happened," said Steve. "It could have been someone else."

"Who?" Jena asked.

"Someone who wanted to protect Brick," said Marcie, suddenly seeing things more clearly. "Someone who thought Melissa was going to spread it all around school that Brick had gotten Rachel pregnant and then had her sent off to have the baby."

Jena nodded. "That would mean it had to be one of Brick's group of friends: Buster, James, Penny, or Kim."

Marcie nodded. "We thought it was most likely James," Marcie said. "We couldn't see Penny or Kim cutting someone's throat. Most women would be too squeamish, and we figured Buster was too weak and disorganized to do anything like that. That left James."

"And he's also the only one who said he didn't see Roger from eight thirty to ten. Maybe that's because he was outside killing Melissa," said Steve.

"I see. Do you have any other evidence?" asked Jena.

Steve and Marcie looked at each other, then shook their heads.

"Do you think James would have murdered someone, a fellow student, just to protect Brick's reputation?"

"He might have. They were a pretty tight group, and most of the fun they had together was being paid for by Brick," said Steve.

"Brick was still paying," said Marcie. "Penny's shop is in one of his buildings. Buster has a job at Brickmore Industries. We don't know what the other two might be getting."

Steve slapped the table. "You know, this review was really valuable. It helped me focus on who would have wanted to help Brick. I think we need to talk to James and find out where he was during the time frame of Melissa's death."

Marcie frowned. "You can do that if you want. But your first priority has to be writing the story using all the information we have so far. You have to get that story done for the *Globe*. Mike Price is going to bring out the story in the local paper any day now. They would scoop you."

"No problem," Steve said with a smile. "I e-mailed my story to the *Globe* this afternoon."

Marcie nodded, impressed by Steve's efficiency. "It would be great if we could get your story in the July or August issue of the magazine. To do that, we'd need it by the end of this month."

"That's in only three weeks," Steve said slowly.

"You know from working on the newspaper that writing is all about meeting deadlines."

"Okay, okay. But I can do both. You'll have the story on time, and I'll keep investigating."

Marcie put down her fork and leaned across the table toward Steve.

"The other reason you might not want to keep going with this investigation is that we now know that there's someone out there willing to commit murder. From now on, you should leave it to the police."

Marcie looked to Jena for support, but she seemed lost in thought.

Steve waved a hand in dismissal. "That's somebody who wanted revenge against Brick. Why would he or she hurt me?"

"To hide their identity, obviously," said Marcie.

Finally Jena spoke. "I'm sorry, Steve, but I think Marcie is right. This case has gotten too dangerous for amateurs—even skilled amateurs—to go poking around in it. Plus, I'm not sure that talking to James will help you very much. Even if James did murder Melissa to help Brick, why would he now kill him?"

Steve was silent for a moment, but Marcie could tell he was struggling to come up with an answer.

"Maybe Brick didn't know who had killed Melissa, but he recently figured it out and was going to tell the police. That would be motive enough for James to kill Brick," Steve said with a smile.

Jena stood up and began to clear the table. "Fair enough, but this isn't a game. I think this is at the stage where it's best left to the police. Listen to Marcie and focus on getting your story done. After all, it's a writer you're trying to become, not a police detective."

Marcie nodded, but one glance at Steve told her that he was not convinced.

"I have almond cookies and ice cream for dessert. Anyone interested?"

Steve's face brightened. "Right here," he said.

Chapter Nineteen

Steve pulled into the driveway at his parents' house after having taken Marcie back to the hotel. They had both been tired, and they hadn't spoken much on the trip. Steve had been reviewing in his mind the questions he planned to ask James Kerr. Normally he would have run his ideas past Marcie, but he knew she didn't approve of his plan to continue the investigation, so silence seemed the wiser course of action.

Steve locked the car and headed for the side door that led into the kitchen and to the stairs down into the basement. *If there were at least a separate entrance, I'd feel better,* he thought. *It would give me the illusion of independence, and the people who come to visit me wouldn't have to pass through the gauntlet of parental observation.*

He had just walked past his parents' car when he felt a crushing pain near the right side of his neck. He cried out and turned. Standing behind him was a figure in a dark, hooded sweatshirt. The figure raised its hand again. Steve put up his left arm to ward off the attack. The blow sent a jolt of lightning through the arm. Steve staggered backward, lost his balance, and fell down hard. He may have blacked out for a moment, because when he was again aware of his surroundings, the figure had disappeared.

A half hour later, Marcie walked into the emergency room. She had received an urgent call from Mrs. Maes right after getting ready for bed, which led to her hurriedly getting dressed again and rushing over to the hospital.

"I shouldn't be doing this," Mrs. Maes said.

"Doing what?"

"Letting you know that Steve is here before I call his mother. It just isn't right."

"I thought you said Steve was attacked right outside his parents' home. How can they not know?"

Mrs. Maes shook her head in amazement. "That poor boy managed to get back in his car and drive over here himself. I don't know how he did it. He must have been in a lot of pain."

"What's wrong with him?"

"A preliminary examination indicated a broken collarbone and a broken arm. He keeps insisting that he wants to talk to you before we call his parents. Follow me in so we can get this out of the way."

They marched quickly down the hall and turned into a room at the right. All that was in it was a hospital bed, a cabinet with some instruments on it that Marcie purposely avoided looking at, and a couple of hard plastic chairs. No one was in the room but Steve.

"I'll give you ten minutes but no more. Then I'm calling your mother."

"Thanks, Mrs. Maes," Steve said.

"What happened to you?" Marcie asked.

"I was attacked. Someone hit me with a pipe or something."

"Did you get a good look at the person?"

"Unfortunately, no. I was hit from behind. By the time I turned around, I was already stunned. I saw part of a face for a few seconds, but I didn't recognize it. I'm betting it was somebody Chief Grundfeld sent to get me off the case."

"Is there anything I can do for you?"

"I was hoping that you might be able to interview James Kerr for me. I think it's important to talk to him now, right after Brick's death, when he might be a little off balance."

"What do you want me to ask him?"

"I want to know where he was during the time frame the police have set for Melissa's murder. Why was he the only one of Brick's gang who didn't report seeing him at the dance?"

"Okay. Anything else?"

"Can you stop by the *Arbella Archives* office and get my bag?" he said, handing her a key. "I'll probably be out of here by the morning, once they've taken X-rays, set my arm, and done whatever they're going to do to the collarbone. So can you call my house tomorrow and see if I'm home? If I am, bring the bag to my house."

"Will do."

Marcie leaned over and gave Steve a kiss on the cheek. "Hope you feel better soon," she said.

Steve tried to smile, but it came out more as a sickly grin.

It wasn't until one o'clock the next day that Marcie was able to see James Kerr. When she'd called, he'd said that he had appointments up until then, which was his lunch hour. He didn't seem willing to sacrifice it until Marcie mentioned that the questions she was going to ask would soon be asked more officially by the police. She wasn't certain whether the police were actually going to do that, but it seemed like a good ploy.

The woman at the front desk took Marcie into the examining area and pointed down to the end of the hall, saying, "The doctor will see you in his office."

Marcie walked down the hall. There were two examination rooms. In one a large Great Dane was sleeping on an operating table; the other appeared to be empty. When she walked into Kerr's office, a brown paper bag sat in the middle of his desk, and he was eating a sandwich while he read a magazine.

"I'm Marcie Ducasse. I called you earlier," she said, putting out her hand.

The doctor took it briefly, then motioned for her to sit down next to the desk.

"So, you want to know about my friendship with Roger Brickmore because you're planning to write an article about him for your magazine."

Marcie knew that wasn't exactly the truth, but it didn't twist things completely into a lie.

"That's right. I know that there was a small group of you who were close friends in high school, and that you've remained close ever since. And I wondered to what extent Mr. Brickmore was responsible for that."

James looked out the window across from his desk for a long moment before answering. "Brick was certainly the one responsible for us forming a group in high school. He picked each of us to be a friend, and then he encouraged us to be a group by always inviting us all to every activity. And he was great for coming up with ideas of things to do." James smiled. "Of course, it didn't hurt that money was no object to him. If he wanted to go skiing, and some of us didn't know how to ski, he paid for us to get lessons, and he kept taking us until we could all ski together."

"Sounds like he ordered you around a bit."

"When you talk about it, it does sound that way. But Brick could be very charming and convincing. He was a bit like a border collie, always interested in herding. You knew he was acting in your own best interest; he wanted you to have fun with the group. And he was willing to do things that the rest of us liked more than he did. For instance, Roger was never much of a swimmer, but several of us liked to go to the beach, so he'd take us to the family beach house for a week in the summer, even though it wasn't his favorite thing to do."

"So basically, the five of you did a lot of things together."

"Certainly."

"You even went to the senior prom together."

"That's right," he said quickly, but a wariness came into his eyes.

"But you didn't hang out together the whole time you were at the prom, did you?"

"No. You have to realize that Kim and I and Penny and Buster had become couples. It didn't start out that way, but I guess over time, we just paired off."

"I see. So you were with Kim the entire night."

"More or less."

"I'm not primarily interested in the murder of Melissa Harrison, but everyone other than you in your group said that they saw Brick during the period of time in which Melissa was killed. So I was just wondering why you didn't see him in that time period. Were you somewhere else?"

"You mean, was I killing Melissa?" He shook his head angrily. "Why would I do that?"

"Because she was threatening to tell everyone that Brick had gotten Rachel pregnant and then refused to marry her."

"I don't know what you're talking about."

"You didn't know then, or now?"

"I didn't know about it until just now when you told me, and I'm pretty sure none of the other people in the group were aware of it."

"Somebody was aware of it, and that somebody chased after Melissa and killed her. It probably wasn't Brick, because too many people saw him in the right time frame. All the other members of your group were seen by each other or by Brick. The only one who disappeared was you."

Kerr reached over and pushed the door shut.

"Okay. This never came up at the time, because the police focused their investigation on Brick and never asked where I was. But the truth is that I was making out with another girl behind the gym. I know that sounds pretty clichéd, but it's true."

"I thought you and Kim were an item," said Marcie.

"That had always been a kind of artificial relationship, based mostly on our seeing a lot of each other. But by our senior year, it had pretty much run its course. I think Kim knew that as much as I did, but she wanted to keep up appearances until the end of high school. We never got together after prom night, and today we aren't even friends."

"So you could produce a witness who would say where you were."

"That's right. Fortunately, I didn't have to, because the police didn't ask. A good thing, because Kim would have been offended and the girl, Becky White, had a boyfriend who was big and had a very bad temper."

"But Becky could say today that you had been with her when Melissa was killed?"

"I suppose so, but I don't know where she is today."

Marcie leaned back in her chair, stymied by James' alibi.

"At the time, who did you think killed Melissa?"

Kerr shook his head. "I had no idea, and I still don't."

"What did Brick say he and Melissa were fighting over if he didn't mention Rachel and the baby?"

"He claimed she'd found out that he was two-timing her with Cindy Gower and was furious."

"Did you and the rest of the group believe that?"

He shrugged. "We had no way of knowing. Melissa didn't hang out with us; none of Brick's girlfriends did. We were in two separate compartments. Brick was always by himself when he went anywhere with us, and there was no double- or triple-dating."

"Why did he do that?"

Kerr paused. "I've thought about that a few times over the years, because it was so peculiar. I guess Brick wanted to be the leader of our group, and if he'd had a girlfriend in the group, he'd have had to share authority with her. I don't think he would have liked that."

Marcie got to her feet.

"Thanks for your help, Dr. Kerr."

He got to his feet as well. More than six feet tall, he towered over her.

"You aren't really planning to write a story about Brick's life, are you?"

Marcie blushed. "Only about the part that involves the murder of Melissa Harrison and the return of her ghost."

"That was scary," the doctor said in a tone that said he meant it. "But I'm quite certain that Brick's death has put an end to it. That was who she intended to kill all along."

"Any idea who's pretending to be the ghost?"

"Somebody who is very angry and very disciplined. She only killed Brick. She could have killed us all."

"That's probably because she thought Brick murdered Melissa."

James sighed. "Lots of people in town thought that at the time. Probably some still do today."

Chapter Twenty

By the time Marcie returned to her room from seeing Kerr and picking up Steve's bag, it was the middle of the afternoon. She'd noticed that there was a daily rhythm to life at the motel. Usually it began to empty out by mid-morning. From the afternoon to early evening, it was almost empty. From ten o'clock at night on, the parking lot began to refill with cars, and it was most crowded between ten and midnight. But Sundays were particularly slow. As Marcie turned around to close the door to her room, Chief Grundfeld pulled up in an unmarked car. He was alone.

He got out of the car and paused to look around. Marcie quickly closed the door, immediately going over to peek out her front window. After looking around some more, as if suspecting that he was being spied upon, Grundfeld went into the motel office. Marcie could see Lisa standing just inside doorway. The chief went inside, and the door closed.

Later, as she thought about it, Marcie was never quite sure why she remained looking out the window. Maybe she was curious as to how long it would take the chief to conduct his business—perhaps scheduling one of his orchestrated raids. Or possibly she was just tired of proofreading and couldn't motivate herself to fire up the laptop and get to work. Whatever the reason, she remained looking out the window. About five minutes later, a car pulled into the lot and a man wearing a suit got out carrying a small suitcase. He looked familiar. When he turned and looked almost directly at her, Marcie recognized him as the man Lisa had been meeting out in the woods. He glanced around, then slowly walked toward the office door and went inside.

I wonder what those three have to do with each other, Marcie thought. *I suspected Lisa of being the ghost without any real evidence, and now I see she's hooked up with the sheriff. I wonder if she's part of some elaborate scheme. Like maybe the chief wanted to eliminate Brickmore, and paid Lisa to do the job along with her male accomplice.* Marcie's mind raced, putting the parts together in a variety of configurations.

A few minutes later, two cars pulled into the parking lot, and four men in suits got out. They immediately ran across the parking lot and tried to get into the office, but the door appeared to be locked. Suddenly, Marcie heard what sounded like fireworks going off. A few seconds later, the man who had gone in with the suitcase appeared in the doorway, holding his right arm as if he were in great pain. He pointed behind him toward the back door out of the office. Two of the men ran inside the office, and Marcie figured they were chasing someone who had left by the back door. The other two turned and ran in the direction of Marcie's room. She hid behind the curtain as they ran past her window and around the side of the building to the back.

Marcie continued watching. The man who was holding his arm sat down in a folding chair outside the door to the office. Lisa came out, handed him a cup of something, and stood next to him. Five minutes later, an ambulance arrived. With Lisa's help, the man got to his feet and went over to meet the EMTs, who immediately had him lie down on a folding stretcher that they pushed inside the ambulance. When they left, Lisa walked back inside the office.

Marcie really wanted to go into the office and talk with Lisa. All she could think of for an excuse was that she was leaving tomorrow, and she just wanted to remind her. That was pretty weak, but Marcie repeated it over and over in her mind as she walked to the office. By the time she reached the door, it sounded pretty convincing to her.

Lisa was standing on a chair in the front corner of the office doing something to a security camera that had been tucked behind a drape. She almost fell off the chair when Marcie said hello.

"You shouldn't be in here. This is a crime scene," Lisa said, getting off the chair and walking toward Marcie as if she intended to throw her out. Instead, she held up a badge. Marcie examined it and saw that Lisa was with the state police.

"What sort of crime?"

"That's none of your business."

"Okay," Marcie said with a smile. "I guess I'll just have to call Mike Price, a reporter for the *Arbella Beacon,* and let him know that a crime has been committed. I don't think you'll find it as easy to throw out a member of the working press."

Lisa sighed, sank down in one of the chairs in the small lobby, and gestured for Marcie to sit across from her.

"How much did you see?"

"I saw Chief Grundfeld come into the office. I saw a man carrying a suitcase come in a few minutes later—the same man you've been having secret meetings with out in the woods in back."

Lisa nodded. "You have been paying attention. And I guess that I haven't been careful enough."

"So what have you been doing, setting up some kind of scam to catch Grundfeld?"

Lisa nodded. "We've known Grundfeld was dirty for quite a while, but we've never had a reliable witness who would testify against him. We decided to set up a sting. I pretended to be the go-between for upper-level drug dealers and several major local suppliers. That man you saw me with is my boss, and he was playing the role of a big-time drug dealer. I'm supposed to take the drugs, pay for them, and pass them along to our local suppliers."

"How is Grundfeld involved?"

"We had somebody on the street slip the word to Grundfeld about me. He came around and more or less said that he would find some excuse to arrest me if I didn't pay him off. Today he was going to get his payoff, and we were going to record it on tape," she said, turning her glance toward the now-exposed camera.

"What went wrong?" asked Marcie.

"Nothing at first. I think we've got a good film of Grundfeld accepting a bribe from me, a self-confessed drug dealer. What we underestimated was how quick and dangerous Grundfeld could be. He heard our backup team come to a screeching halt in the parking lot, and before we could react, he locked the door and had his gun out. My boss tried to draw his, and Grundfeld shot him. He's lucky it was only his arm."

"And then Grundfeld took off out the back door," Marcie added.

"And into the woods. Eventually we'll find him. There's really nowhere that he can go. We've got his office, home, and hangouts covered. And his bank account is frozen. He's on foot, so it's only a matter of time."

"Accepting a bribe won't put him away for a long time, will it?"

"Being he's a police officer, it will be a few years. And bribery is just the beginning. Once people see that he's vulnerable, we'll find out about all sorts of other illegal activities in which he's been involved."

"Your investigation wouldn't have happened to come up with anything concerning the ghost of Melissa Harrison or the death of Roger Brickmore?"

Lisa laughed. "Ghosts are outside our jurisdiction. All I can tell you about the Brickmore case is that Grundfeld didn't kill him. We've had him on around-the-clock surveillance for the last month."

Marcie got to her feet. "Why did you want me to leave early tomorrow?"

"You're the only person renting here whom we know for sure isn't involved in local crime in some way. The scam was originally set up to happen on Monday, and we didn't want you getting hurt. But at the same time, we couldn't risk telling you what's going on. Then, for some reason that nobody has bothered to tell me yet, it got moved back to today."

Marcie nodded. "Well, good luck catching Grundfeld. I have a feeling he's going to be harder to apprehend than you think."

"We'll get him eventually. They all make mistakes."

When she got back to her room, Marcie called Steve.

"You've got to help me escape from this prison," he said. "My mother is down here every five minutes asking me if I'm all right. She's driving me crazy."

"I won't help you escape, but I'll come over and keep you company for a few hours."

"The next best thing," Steve said eagerly.

Twenty minutes later Marcie knocked on the side door of Steve 's house. A short, round older woman opened the door.

"You must be Marcie," she exclaimed as if she'd been waiting her entire life to meet her.

Marcie said she was and that she was there to see Steve.

"I'll take you right down there. He's really in no condition to even get out of bed yet. Follow me."

Marcie followed her down a stairway in the corner of the kitchen that led to the cellar. Sometime in the past, the basement had been finished with knotty pine paneling that gave it a dark, rather rustic look. The stairs led you into an open area that had a sofa and one chair. In one corner was a half bath and in the other was a small bedroom where she saw Steve lying with a plastic donut around his neck and a cast on his arm. She put his bag next to his bed.

"Thanks," he said softly.

"The poor boy!" his mother exclaimed, as if shocked all over again every time she saw him in his diminished condition.

"I feel a lot better than I look," Steve said to Marcie.

"He thinks he can go back to school tomorrow. I tried to tell him that it's better to rest up for a few days than start back too soon and have a relapse."

"I don't think you have a relapse from broken bones, Mom," Steve said.

His mother squeezed his leg to humor him. Marcie wasn't taking any bets that Steve would be going back to school the next day.

"Well, I'll leave the two of you alone for now," his mother said. "You'll stay for supper, won't you, Marcie?"

"I'm not . . ."

"You won't have to eat upstairs with Sam and me. I'll bring plates down for you and Steve. He can't manage the stairs very well yet anyway."

"Please stay," Steve said in a pleading voice.

"I'll be happy to stay," Marcie said.

Mrs. Rostow beamed and left the room.

When Marcie was sure that Steve's mother was out of earshot, she asked, "So how are you really?"

Steve shrugged, and a spasm of pain went over his face. "Guess I shouldn't do that with a broken collarbone."

"Does it hurt all the time?"

He shook his head. "Only when I move a certain way. And the arm doesn't bother me. Fortunately, it wasn't a serious fracture. They gave me painkillers, but they make me sleep all the time. I'm trying to get along with just extra-strength aspirin."

"Can you really go to school tomorrow?"

"Technically, I probably could. My left arm is broken, and I'm a righty. That means I could still drive and write on the board. But I don't think I'll be up to it by then. I'm just saying that to lay the groundwork with Mom for going back the next day. She'll be so happy when I stay home tomorrow that she won't object if I go in on Tuesday."

"Pretty clever."

Steve frowned. "But pretty sad that I'm still trying to outsmart my parents at twenty-seven."

"Some people say it never stops, no matter what your age," Marcie said. "But I think I can cheer you up with some news."

"About the ghost?"

"Not exactly, but you'll still be happy to hear it because it involves your friend Grundfeld ending up in very hot water."

"That sounds just like what the doctor ordered."

When Marcie finished her story about the afternoon's events, Steve leaned back carefully and smiled.

"Getting rid of Grundfeld will be good for Arbella. Whoever gets the job next won't have the same combination of unscrupulousness and smarts that he had."

"Unfortunately, none of that helps us with the ghost story," said Marcie. "I don't really think James murdered Melissa. We could always ask the police to check with the girl he claimed to be with at the time. But I have a feeling that she'll corroborate his story."

"I always thought James was a long shot," said Steve. "So who do we have left?"

"Actually, the problem is that we've got two questions: who killed Melissa and who killed Brick? If the person who killed Brick did it in revenge for the murder of Melissa, then we've got two different killers."

"And one of them would be Brick, if he killed Melissa."

"But if he didn't, then we're back to looking for two other people."

"I think we should follow Jena's advice and write the story with what we've got, even if it is open-ended. Now that Grundfeld is out of the picture there may be more action in solving this case, and we can always make changes up to the deadline," said Marcie.

"I certainly won't be able to do much for a few days," Steve admitted. "So I guess I'll get writing."

Having run out of conversation on the murders, Steve suggested that maybe they could play chess. Over the next hour they played two games, each winning one. After suggesting one each was a good way to stay friends, Steve settled back and looked at Marcie.

"This morning I was lying here and thinking about my life."

"That sounds ominous," Marcie said with a grin.

"Well, you know, I guess that attack rattled me more than I thought. It also got me thinking about my priorities and what I should do next."

"Have you made any decisions?"

"For all the complaining I do about it, I actually enjoy teaching, and I'm pretty good at it. I've never really admitted that to myself, because I always thought that I should be a writer. Now I'm starting to think that teaching can be an equally worthwhile profession, and maybe I'm even better at it than writing."

"You may influence more people as a teacher than as a writer," Marcie agreed.

"And like you said, I can always write articles for magazines and keep working on the *Archives.* Who knows what might come up? If writing ever looks like it's going to really amount to something, I can always make that decision then."

"Sure. Lots of people write part time and have day jobs."

"I've also been thinking about what you said last night at Jena's about my getting a place of my own. I haven't been really honest with myself about why I haven't left here. The real reason is that it would hurt my mom, and that makes it difficult for me. But I think it's time that she recognized I'm a grown-up, and to be an adult I have to live in my own place."

"I'm sure she'll be upset at first, but it's not like you'll be moving across the country."

"Just across Arbella," Steve said with a grin.

"It sounds like being attacked was just what you needed to put your life in order."

"You know what they say about clouds and silver linings."

Chapter Twenty-one

Marcie returned to the motel. It was starting to feel like home, which worried her a little bit. She parked her car directly in front of the door so that loading up would be easier in the morning. There was a light on in the office, and Marcie was tempted to go over there and see if Lisa was still pretending to be the manager. The owners, assuming that they weren't involved in the drug deal, were going to have to find a new manager soon.

Marcie opened the door to her room and stepped inside. The place smelled different, and she paused with her hand on the switch that turned on the bedroom table lamp. Before she could react, an arm came around her throat and she was pulled into the room, the door slamming shut behind her. The arm tightened, and she felt the blood pounding in her head like it was going to explode. Just as she was about to lose consciousness, the pressure lessened.

"This is a choke hold. I can cut off the supply of arterial blood to your brain and leave you a vegetable if I want to.

Do you understand me?" a man's voice said. Marcie couldn't speak, and when she tried to nod her head, his arm was in the way. He must have felt her head go up and down, because he loosened his grip some more.

"I'm going to let go of you and turn on the light. I have a gun, and if you try to run, I won't hesitate to kill you. Do you understand?"

This time Marcie's head nod was more obvious. The arm disappeared from around her neck, and a split second later the light went on. Marcie found herself facing Charlie Grundfeld, who was holding a gun in his hand and pointing it directly at the center of her body.

Grundfeld looked hot and tired. His shirt was ripped, and his face was scratched. Mud was smeared all over his pants, and somewhere along the way he'd lost his sports coat, so she could clearly see the holster on his belt.

"Who are you?" he asked.

"Marcie Ducasse."

Grundfeld stared at her for a long moment, then nodded in recognition.

"I saw you the other night at the hospital. You were with that Rostow kid. You must be that magazine writer he got to come out here."

"I didn't think you spotted me," said Marcie.

Grundfeld smiled coldly. "I don't miss much, and I never forget a face. That's a real gift in my line of work."

Marcie almost asked whether he meant his work as a cop or as a criminal, but she decided against it.

"And just this morning, one of my officers, Jena Conway, was suggesting that I should run you out of town."

Marcie wondered why Jena would do that.

"Well, Marcie Ducasse, for the next fifteen minutes or

so, we're going to be roommates, so why don't you sit on the bed right there."

Grundfeld waved the gun, indicating that she should sit on the foot of the double bed while he settled down in the chair right across from her.

"Now, isn't this nice?" he said with a smile.

"Looks like you've had a tough afternoon, running away from the state police," said Marcie.

The man reached up and touched the scratch across his cheek.

"Yeah, at first I had to put some distance between me and them. But I always figured on doubling back. I know this part of the world, so I ran until I reached a stream, then I took off my shoes and walked in the stream and doubled back here. I figured this would be the last place anyone would look for me. I wanted the room on the end because it's more private. I didn't know who was staying here. I figured it was probably some hooker. But I'm glad to see that it's someone respectable, someone who has more to lose."

"What did you have to do with Melissa's ghost?"

Grundfeld looked genuinely surprised. "Nothing at all, except that I'd like to find the little witch who's playing that game."

"What about the attack on Steve Rostow? Didn't you do that?"

The chief shook his head. "Sorry, that wasn't me either, although I'd like to thank whoever laid out that annoying punk."

Marcie frowned. A car pulled into the lot, and Grundfeld, keeping one eye on her, went to the window and peeked out around the drape. It must not have been who he was looking for, because he returned to his chair.

"Are you expecting company?" Marcie asked.

"I'm expecting a ride. It's time for me to get outta Dodge."

"You'll be giving up a lot."

Grundfeld shrugged. "I've already got a small fortune stashed away in offshore banks. I haven't wasted my time as police chief."

"How did you ever get to be chief in the first place?"

"You know, I could take offense at your tone, little lady. I happen to be a pretty good cop. But you're right—without a college degree, I'd never have made it to the top if not for my friend Roger Brickmore."

"That's right, somebody told me that you went to high school together. How come you weren't part of his gang?"

"Guess I'm not a joiner. Anyway, those guys were all losers who needed Brick to make them into something. I always was something. Brickmore and I were equals. Sometimes I did what he asked, other times I didn't."

"But he helped you get the job as chief. Why did he do that?"

"He owed me."

"For what?"

"That's enough questions for now, little lady."

As Marcie sat there without speaking, her anxiety grew. Was all of Grundfeld's friendliness just a way of controlling her? She'd read about serial killers who used their charm to lull victims into a false sense of security so they don't make trouble.

"You won't be happy living outside the country for the rest of your life," Marcie said sharply, hoping to prove that she wouldn't be deceived by his nice manner.

"I don't plan to be. One thing about being a cop is that you develop lots of contacts with criminals. I know some guys who do a pretty good job setting up false identities for people. Once things calm down, I'll get in touch with one of them and become a new person. Then I'll come back to the States."

"Where will you go?"

"I'm getting a little tired of New England. Maybe I'll try somewhere along the Pacific coast."

There was a loud rap on the door. Grundfeld jumped, and his finger tightened on the trigger enough to make Marcie think it was all over. Grundfeld stood up and motioned for her to come over and stand in front of him.

"You get the door. Remember I'll be behind you with a gun pointed right at your spine."

Marcie got off the bed and walked past Grundfeld. She jumped slightly when she felt him press the gun into her back. She opened the door. Jena Conway stood in the doorway.

"Jena," Marcie said cheerfully.

Before she could say more, the chief pulled her out of the doorway and opened the door wide. "Get in here, Conway."

Jena slowly entered, her eyes moving restlessly around the room.

"I told you to park in front and blink the lights, and I'd come out to you."

"I didn't want to be that conspicuous."

The chief ran a hand nervously over his bald head. "Now we're going to have to kill her," he said, pointing at Marcie. "She's seen you. I was going to tie her up and dump her in a closet. By the time anyone found her I'd be out of the country. But now that won't work because she can finger you."

"Let me take care of it, Chief," Jena said softly. She

reached behind her back, and in her right hand a knife with a long, thin blade appeared. "This way there won't be any noise."

Confused for a moment, Grundfeld pointed his gun at a space between the two women. Jena took a step toward Marcie and raised the knife. Marcie took a step back on trembling legs.

"Wait. I'll hold her," Grundfeld said, holstering his gun.

Jena turned to the right and faced the police chief.

"This is for Melissa," she said softly as she plunged the knife into his chest.

Grundfeld backpedaled furiously, making a wheezing sound in his throat. Jena came toward him once again with the knife raised, but Grundfeld still had some life in him. He pulled the automatic, and just as Jena thrust the knife into him a second time, he managed to fire one shot. Jena spun backward and fell to the floor.

Stunned and deafened by the sound of the gunshot, Marcie stood there without moving. The door to the room opened, and a figure appeared there. Marcie couldn't see the face, but she had long hair and was wearing a dress. She looked into the room, and then Marcie saw her head nod as if she was in agreement with what had just happened. Then she stepped back from the doorway and disappeared. Was it Melissa, or the girl from the soda machine, or someone else? Marcie couldn't tell.

She reached into the pocket of her jacket and took out her phone. With trembling fingers, she punched in 9-1-1. The thought came to her that maybe all the police on duty were right here in her room already. She began to giggle, but stopped when the operator asked her to describe her emergency.

Chapter Twenty-two

Over a week had passed, and Marcie was again pulling into Arbella. It was a Saturday, and she had little trouble driving through town to the hospital. She got a good spot near the building and walked into the lobby, where Steve was waiting for her. The foam collar was no longer around his neck, and all that showed of his attack was the cast on his arm.

"Hi, Steve," Marcie said, giving him a quick hug. "How're you feeling?"

"Pretty good. I went back to work on Wednesday. Took me a little longer than I expected. But everything is pretty much going along as it should, according to the doctor."

"You said that Jena is getting out of the hospital today."

"Yeah. They're going to transfer her to the county jail's infirmary."

"I thought she was a goner when Grundfeld shot her."

"She was lucky that the bullet missed all of her vital organs. Well, at least she was lucky in one way, but if she gets the full sentence for two murders, I'm not sure she wouldn't be better off dead."

"You said that she asked to see us."

Steve nodded. "The district attorney didn't have any trouble with that, since she's signed a confession."

"Why does she want to talk to us?"

"I guess Jena thought of us as her friends, and she wants to explain why she did what she did."

"She really didn't have to bother," said Marcie, still angry at being fooled and manipulated by Jena.

"But you would like to know, wouldn't you?" Steve asked.

Marcie gave a guilty smile. "Yeah, I guess I would."

They took the elevator up to the fifth floor and walked down the hall to a room with a police officer sitting outside. He asked to see their driver's licenses for identification, then nodded that they could enter the room.

Marcie was surprised at how good Jena looked. Her color was fine, and she smiled as if greeting them somewhere around town.

"Thanks for coming, Marcie, and you too, Steve." She studied Marcie. "Are you okay?"

"Why do you ask?"

"Seeing all that violence up close must have been very disturbing."

"I'm fine," Marcie said, not willing to admit that she hadn't slept through the night since the event. That had happened to her before. It always seemed to fade away with time.

Jena kept looking at her. "Get some counseling if you need it."

"What did you want to tell us?" Marcie asked impatiently. She didn't want Jena thinking they were still friends after what she had done.

Jena paused and looked out the window. "I wanted to explain why I killed Brickmore and Grundfeld."

"Are you going to tell us why you pretended to be Melissa's ghost?" Steve asked.

She nodded. "My mother was Rachel Carpenter. I'm the child she had by Roger Brickmore. Mom worked in the house of my great-aunt Sarah. She treated my mother like a slave because she thought my mother needed to be punished for being a 'fallen woman.' We had almost no money, because whatever my grandmother sent for our care was kept by Sarah."

"Didn't your grandmother try to put a stop to that?"

Jena shook her head. "She never talked to my mother again, and never even met me. She considered us both to be dead. Well, she's dead now, and good riddance."

"Is Sarah dead as well?"

"Yes, six years ago. Fortunately, the woman was too stupid to leave a will, and it turned out that I was her next of kin, so I got most of her estate. My mother had died at thirty, when her car hit a tree. I've always considered it a suicide. I used that money I got from Aunt Sarah to change my name and to start a new life here after I hatched my plan."

"Why did you want to avenge Melissa?" asked Steve.

"Because she was my mother's only friend. My mother wrote to her and told her that she was pregnant by Brick but that he wouldn't marry her."

"Like I told you at your condo, Brick was willing to marry her," said Marcie. "It was your grandmother who put a stop to it. Talk to Reverend Carstairs. He was there."

Jena frowned. "Well, maybe Brick wasn't as irresponsible as I thought. But you can't tell me that there wasn't a single time in the next twenty years when he could have gotten in touch with my mother or me. Anyway, I also wanted to kill him because I thought he had killed Melissa.

"When my mother wrote to Melissa to describe how miserable her life was, she got a reply from Melissa written on the day of the senior prom. Melissa said that she planned to talk to Brick, and if he wouldn't go public with being the child's father, she would expose him to everyone at school."

"We were right, then," said Marcie. "That is what they argued about at the prom."

"You can imagine what my mother thought when she happened to see a Maine newspaper that had a short piece on Melissa's murder. My mother immediately thought Brick had killed Melissa so he could go on denying my mother and her baby."

"But he didn't," said Marcie.

Jena shook her head. "And maybe I wouldn't have killed him if I'd known, but I'd always assumed my mother was right. Even when I got the job here and went through all the police evidence, Brick was still the most likely suspect."

"When did you start to think differently?" asked Marcie.

"Grundfeld said to me that the Brickmore killing was all because of a baby. Now, no one knew about the baby in Arbella except for Brick and his father, my mother and grandmother, and the minister. None of the gang were ever told about it. That got me wondering how Grundfeld could know unless Brick had told him. I started thinking how dependent Brick seemed to be on Grundfeld, and how Grundfeld could say almost anything to Brick and get away with it. I figured that on the night of the prom, after the fight with Melissa, it was Grundfeld that Brick told about the fix he was in, and Grundfeld told him not to worry, and he'd take care of it. And he did, by murdering Melissa. When I looked back over the police files, nobody had checked on Grundfeld because he wasn't part of Rogers 'gang' of particular friends."

"I understand why you killed Brickmore and Grundfeld, but why did you attack the others?" asked Steve.

Jena shrugged. "I didn't know which of them had told the truth about what happened that night and which had lied to protect Brick. Remember, I started out thinking he was the killer. I thought that if I could shake things up enough, someone might come forward and tell the truth, so the case could be reopened."

Marcie snapped her fingers. "Now I've got it. I know why what Buster told me about recognizing the ghost as Melissa bothered me. He never saw a resemblance for himself. You said that Grundfeld pointed out the similarity to him, but Buster said that Grundfeld laughed when Buster claimed the girl was the ghost of Melissa. So someone else who was in that hospital room must have told him, and the only other person there, even before Grundfeld arrived, was you."

"Yes. In order to get Melissa's murder out in the open, I had to have people recognize the ghost as being her, so I started with poor, impressionable Buster. My wig and makeup made me look somewhat like Melissa, based on her yearbook picture, but there was no guarantee that anyone would recognize her. I told Buster what he saw, to be sure that the correct story started to be spread around. I actually told Penny that I was Melissa's ghost at the time I attacked her, because she hasn't got the brains of a turnip. James was so far down the line that I let him figure it out for himself."

"Why did Brick stop by the side of the road when you were there?" asked Steve.

"Because I wasn't dressed up as the ghost. I had on a nice dress, like I was going somewhere and happened to have a flat tire. He never suspected, and that made it so easy."

"And you also attacked Steve," Marcie said, giving her a hard stare.

"I'm sorry, Steve. I tried slipping you information all along because Brick was doing such a good job keeping it out of the paper. I figured your story would at least do something. But finally I couldn't wait that long. I wanted justice now. Then, after I killed Brick, I was afraid that the two of you might dig deep enough to find out about me, so I tried to discourage you from continuing the investigation. I knew Marcie was ready to stop, but Steve, you are like a pit bull. I knew you would never give up unless you were hurt."

Steve smiled. "Thanks for the compliment."

"But I figured that if I could put you out of action for a couple of days, I'd be able to take care of Grundfeld and get out of town before anyone knew who I was." She smiled regretfully at Marcie. "If Grundfeld hadn't picked your room to hide in, I would have gotten away with it. I'd have had my revenge, and no one would ever have known the ghost's identity."

"And now you'll have to spend years in prison," said Marcie.

Jena nodded. "But for me it's worth it. Now my mom and Melissa have justice. When I get out of prison, I can start over again and be a law-abiding person. I'm pretty young. I'll make it. I always knew there was a good chance that I'd be caught. I look at this as just the final phase of getting justice."

"I'm glad you can see it that way," said Marcie, wondering whether the ability to justify to oneself the most abhorrent acts was evidence of insanity.

When Marcie and Steve left the hospital, they walked to the parking lot together, finally stopping by Marcie's car.

"I'll look forward to receiving your story," Marcie said. "I saw the piece they ran last week in the *Globe*. It was excellent."

"Thanks. I think they're going to want a follow-up piece when the trial starts. I'll have the article for *Roaming New England* to you in a couple of weeks. I won't put in a lot of what Jena said just now, because it might affect the trial. But I will briefly tell the reader there are strong suspicions that Jena did it and why."

Marcie nodded. "The whole thing is rather sad, really. The one person who deserves the most blame is Rachel's mother, who purposely let her daughter think that Brick didn't love her. It shows how one mean, malicious person's actions has consequences that ripple down through the years."

"By the way," Steve said, "I wanted to ask you, how much of the supernatural do I have to put in the story? It seems to me that this is a pretty straightforward piece about crime and revenge."

Marcie thought about the figure who had appeared to her in the doorway of the motel, and she put her arm around Steve's shoulder. "Let me tell you a little story. Maybe things won't sound quite so straightforward to you when I'm done."